Slave Lover

Slave Lover

Marco Vassi

OPEN ROAD

INTEGRATED MEDIA

NEW YORK

Copyright © 1993 by Marco Vassi

ISBN 978-1-4976-4084-9

This edition published in 2014 by Open Road Integrated Media, Inc.
345 Hudson Street
New York, NY 10014
www.openroadmedia.com

Slave Lover

Introduction

Were the Sixties put on earth so that Marco Vassi could happen? Or was Marco Vassi put on earth so that the Sixties could happen? To read his classic works of erotic fiction and his masterpiece of autobiographical fiction, THE STONED APOCALYPSE, is to realize that the man and the era were created out of the same fire and primordial elements. It is not, however, enough to say that Marco Vassi was a child of his age. It could just as accurately be said that the age was Marco Vassi's fantasy, a fantasy so intense and compelling that it is impossible to read any of his books in one sitting: one must either jump into a cold shower, relieve oneself sexually, or go for a long contemplative walk to reflect on the profundity of his insights into human behavior.

Vassi had done many things before he became a writer, but writing was not one of them except for some translations from Chinese and critiques of manuscripts submitted to a literary agency where he was employed for a few years. He had also tried numerous identities on for size as he acted out and lived out the experiences that were to pour from his mind like water raging over the spillway of a dam. When in the late 1960s "Fred" Vassi announced that he was embarking on a journey, his friends knew that it was not to a place but to a state of mind.

The state of mind was what came to be known as the Sixties, and anyone seeking to live in that state must enter it through the vision of the author of these works. In cartographic terms it was a journey from the East Coast to California, a trip that resonates with meaning for every student of the American Experience. Speaking metaphorically, however, it was a trip into the heart of life, love, laughter, horror, and sweet pain. Fred Vassi came back Marco Vassi, *having recreated himself in the name of the intrepid voyager to the ends of the known world hundreds of years ago.*

Heart fecund with all that had happened to him, he started writing the work that was eventually to become THE STONED APOCALYPSE, *a book that captured in coruscating words what others of his generation were capturing so brilliantly in music.*

With no source of regular income he tried his hand at what were then popularly known as sex novels, a genre of tame pornography that pandered to the fantasies of repressed males still mired in postwar inhibition. With the wide-eyed innocence and self-deprecating humor that characterized every venture he undertook, he showed them to me, his friend and a fledgling literary agent. He merely hoped to raise a few dollars with them. I told him that they were the most incredibly arousing works of erotic literature since Henry Miller, and arranged for them to be brought out by Olympia Press, Miller's publisher. Critics and reviewers confirmed my assessment. What distinguished his books from the rest of the pack was the application of Vassi's intelligence. He knew that the mind is the most erotic organ of all. He termed this fusion of mind and sex organs "Metasex."

For Marco Vassi, the liberation of sexual emotions, paralleling the liberation of so many others in the late 1960s and early 1970s, promised a new age of beauty, love, and honesty, and he lived his vision to the hilt—quite literally. For a long while it seemed to him impossible that this vision did not rest on the bedrock of reality.

But, in the words of Robert Frost, nothing gold can stay. The bloody hand of Vietnam and the corrupt fist of the Nixon presidency crushed the fragile beauty of the Flower Generation. The unbridled commercialism that became the 1980s captured and exploited the butterflies of Woodstock, enriching half of them and killing the other half with sex, drugs, and rock 'n' roll. Finally, the horror of a new scourge, AIDS, visited death upon the bodies of those who had dreamed of eternal love, irresponsible fun, and self-realization. It was then that Marco Vassi awoke from his dream of the Sixties. When he did, the virus had entered his blood. The first malady of any consequence to come along, in his case pneumonia, conquered his defenseless immune system and made short work of him.

Marco Vassi's body died, but not the body of his work, which lives again in these new editions. Like a rainbow over a bleak landscape, his dream of the Sixties shimmers above the depressing, sordid, and tragic decades that succeeded his. And, ultimately, it triumphs over them.

Richard Curtis

1

When she woke up, she was tied facedown on a table and a man, she could not see who it was, was fucking her slowly and rhythmically in the ass. Her surprise was less at her total situation than at the fact that she was able to take the stranger's cock with such ease. She had only been ass-fucked twice before, and each time it had been too painful for her to bear. Now, there was a kind of pleasurable warmth, a deep loosening in her bowels, a tingling vibration which spread into her thighs and stroked the inside of her cunt. She realized that she was moist between the legs, and suffered a slight astonishment that she was capable of being turned on in such an essentially terrifying position.

Constance was a quick-minded woman, twenty-seven years old, a free-lance writer who had begun to make a reputation among some of the more solid publications. Her articles had appeared in *Esquire*, the *Village Voice*, *Harper's*, *Cosmopolitan*, *Ms.*, *Forum*, and several dozen other, smaller magazines and newspapers. She had a wide-ranging intelligence, and her pieces covered everything from Middle East politics to new tendencies in American religious thought. Her latest interest had been in something that most people consider a dead issue: the white-slave trade.

The word "white" was a misnomer in the current phase of that iniquitous business. It had been accurate during the previous century when white women were kidnapped specifically for use in Arab harems and whorehouses, but the trade had evolved into an equal opportunity employer and whisked women away without regard for race, color, nationality or religion. Constance had first formulated the idea that slavers still operated after being puzzled by a pattern of disappearances she had perceived while doing research with local newspapers for another project. A 22-year-old from a small town in Kansas in April, a 19-year-old from Iowa in May, a 16-year-old from Oregon also in May, and so on. No single disappearance was enough to cause more than a local stir, but after going over a number of papers for the previous year, she discovered that more than 100 women had mysteriously vanished.

The man above her now began to move with greater speed and power. She felt his thick thighs slapping against the back of her legs, his groin grinding into her buttocks, his cock insinuating its way deep into her asshole, pushing, pulsing, raping. His breath was hot and raspy in her ear and there was a thin sheet of sweat between his hairy chest and the smooth skin between her shoulder blades.

"It feels like he's been fucking me for hours," she thought, and wondered what it was all about, whether there was anyone else in the room—she assumed they were in a room—or whether anyone else had fucked her.

She opened her eyes.

"Hey, this bitch is waking up!" said the man above her. "I told you I wanted her unconscious for the whole thing."

"Sorry, Mr. Eliot," said a silky voice somewhere to the side other. "I'll take care of it at once."

No more than a few seconds passed before Constance felt a sharp pin prick in her right arm. It took only an instant for her to realize that she was being injected with a hypodermic. She cried out briefly but that only brought a heavy palm down across the side of her face. The blow stunned her and she felt the salt taste of blood at the corner of her lips.

"Shut up, cunt!" the man above her said. "You're spoiling my fun."

The liquid was squeezed into her arm and almost at once she started to go under. She lay there for several minutes, hovering between consciousness and sleep as the man above her began to fuck her again. The relaxation induced by the drug had an odd effect, however, in that it sensitized her skin. Her peculiar mental state made her dramatically aware of each square millimeter of flesh. The man's cock felt huge and hot in her ass. She thought she could feel the vein on the underbelly of the massive tool as he slid in and out. He brought his cock out to the very tip and held it there and her asshole quivered with emptiness, and then he shoved in again. She could feel the rim of the head, the relatively narrow section behind it, and then the slow, magnificent swelling to the thick base. At the end of his thrust, his bristly pubic hair pressed against her ass cheeks.

"I want to fuck her when she's really dead," she heard the man say just before a black veil fell over her mind.

When she woke up again the first sensation was of pain. She was blindfolded, so she couldn't see what was being done. She had to feel the situation from within to make out what they were doing to her. She took an inventory of her body. First her ankles. Obviously tied. Her legs seemed to be pulled wide. The muscles on the insides of her thighs were sore with straining. Her knees trembled slightly. She was so fatigued from strain and so cloudy from the aftereffects of the drug that it took a while to figure out her position. She was lying on her back, her wrists tied with her arms stretched as wide as they would go. Her legs were pulled apart and lifted up. Anyone standing in front of her would have a perfect view of her naked cunt and asshole.

Her asshole throbbed. There was no way of telling how long the man had fucked her. And her nipples ached terribly. She thought it might be because they had been pinched too hard, but then realized that the pinching was still going on. Something was attached to them, something applying a sharp, hard pressure.

"There she is," she heard a voice say. It sounded like it belonged to the same man who had injected her earlier.

"And she's really a slave?" another voice replied.

"Kidnapped, bound, and held prisoner against her will, all in classic style," the man she now was beginning to refer to as Smoothy replied. "She should just be waking up now, so anything you do or say to her will be registered completely. You may induce any terror you desire. But she's new and we aren't ready to snuff her yet, so be careful you don't damage the goods."

"Can I fist-fuck her?" the first man asked.

"Be my guest," Smoothy told him. "Hurt her all you like but don't break any bones."

"This is fantastic," her soon-to-be tormentor said. "She's beautiful."

"It's what you're paying for. She's also very intelligent, and so anyone interested in the psychological aspects of her bondage will have quite a treat. But I gather the impression you're not interested in anything that subtle."

"No. I just want to jam my fist up her cunt and fuck her ass and fuck her mouth."

"A word of caution here. I advise that you use one of the rubber bafflers if you want to abuse her mouth. Otherwise there is nothing to restrain her from

3

biting your cock clean off. A woman in her situation has nothing to lose, so she might shed some of her more decent qualities."

"If she did that . . ." the second man began.

"If she did that," Smoothy interrupted, "you would issue a cry of excruciating pain and deadly shock and be dead within minutes." There was a pause. "There will be an attendant nearby should you need help or if you get carried away. Have a pleasant experience."

For Constance, the conversation held a certain bizarre fascination. It was as though she were watching a movie and getting involved in the plot and characters and wondering what would happen next. The fact that whatever happened would be happening to her didn't strike home until she felt the first contact at her cunt. That a strange man that she couldn't see was going to shove his fist inside her, that he would derive pleasure from hurting her, killing her, and that she was absolutely helpless, was so extraordinary an occurrence that it seemed she must be dreaming.

Her mind sped back to the circumstances which led her to this ridiculous and terrible predicament. Once she had accepted that the disappearances of young women formed a pattern, it only took a small leap of imagination to conclude that it was the result of an organized group. She was unable for a while to grasp the full implications of that, but when she did, her heart almost stopped. She became convinced, in her excitement of discovery, that slavers were at work kidnapping women to be sold as erotic objects around the world. And if she could uncover the story, document it, and publish it, her reputation would be permanently established. She would be automatically catapulted into the ranks of the great journalists of the century.

The problem was how to find them. And to do that, she enlisted the aid of a long-term lover, Chet Cooper, who was a computer designer with a Ph.D. in mathematics from Stanford. She had known Chet for four years, and over that period of time had developed an easy cycle of getting together. They spent half the weekends of the year together, and usually one night out of every week, and took ten-day vacations whenever they could both get away from work at the same time. After she had known him for a year, she stopped seeing any other men, because Chet satisfied her completely. His mind was quite the equal of hers, he was five inches taller than her five-foot-seven, and he was a skilled lovemaker. When his cock sang inside her, she spread her cunt to the heavens and humped herself into oblivion in her effort to get him lodged ever more deeply in her belly. She loved the taste of his sperm. And he would sometimes eat her for hours, even slipping strawberries in her pussy and sucking them out, or pouring wine into her hot hole and drinking it slowly, making her twitch with abandon. The one thing she had never been able to enjoy was ass-fucking, but Chet was willing to forgo that.

4

"After all, we should save something for when we're married," he told her.

"I'm not sure I want to get married," she always replied. "We have it so good as it is. Why take the chance of spoiling it?"

"Because I want us to live together and have kids," he said.

"I don't want anything to stand in the way of my career," was her constant comment.

She had gone to Chet with the problem of the disappearances and he had run all the data into one of his computers and found a possible hard pattern.

"But this is only statistical," he had warned. "If there are men doing this, then their choices may be based on whimsy as much as on plan."

"But it's at least something to go on."

He had used the longitude and latitude and times of all the places and dates on which women disappeared and come to the conclusion that the next happening would be in four days in a town called Glens Falls in New York State. He and Constance surmised that the men were probably traveling around in a van, picking the girls up and transferring them to another vehicle, then cooling off for a week and moving onto the next town.

"Now that you have a probable time and location—and I emphasize that it's only probable—what are you going to do?" he had asked.

"Go there. Watch. Read the local papers. See if I can see anything suspicious."

"Be careful," he had warned, and then had hoisted up her skirt, pulled down her panties, and fucked her from behind as she bent over one of the computer terminals. It had been a bizarre experience to feel the juices running from her pulsing cunt down her thighs, to listen to her own rasping grunts of bestial pleasure, as the most sophisticated of human technology purred warmly under her belly and printouts as indecipherable as some ancient cuneiform writing danced before her eyes.

The following day she went to Glens Falls where she spent an uneventful forty-eight hours before the town was stirred by the news of a young woman's disappearance. However, it was generally thought that she had run off with a disreputable musician who sometimes passed through town and the matter died down quickly.

Constance wrote a long and powerful article then, outlining the details of her discoveries and theories, mentioning the use of computers to help her track the story down, and ending with the predicted kidnapping in Glens Falls. To her chagrin, no one would buy it and she ended selling it to the *National Enquirer* which chopped it to a thousand words and ran it as a scare feature.

She considered the matter at an end until, one evening, as she was returning to her apartment from having run out to buy cigarettes, a hand came down over her mouth and her nose was filled with the suffocating smell of chloroform. She didn't regain consciousness until that moment when she awoke to find a man fucking her vigorously in the ass.

"Gonna ream you good, baby," the man in front of her was now saying.

One finger went into her cunt and moved around. Constance felt her juices beginning to flow. It was absurd that her body should respond in this way when her mind wanted to keep at bay. Or did it? There was a part of her which held that she should not want to be in the situation she was in, but another voice pointed out that since she was indeed trapped there, it would be foolish to do anything but drain the situation of all it had to offer. She didn't want to suffer or be damaged or be killed, but perhaps offering no resistance was the best way to insure her chances of surviving.

The man now had two fingers inside her.

"Gettin' wet," he crooned. "Little cunt is gettin' wet. Yah, that's what I like. I love it when they go wild."

He had pulled his fingers back and when he slipped them back in, the number had doubled. Four fingers entered her, the width of the slab of flesh running from the top to the bottom of her cunt. But when he had gone into the widening slit up to the first knuckles, he suddenly gave a twist which made Constance gasp. He turned his hand sideways and now the full breadth of the four fingers plunged into her distended hole. Once he had established himself so far, he began to move more energetically. He pushed in and pulled out with increasing speed and force. Until he was finger-fucking her with full vehemence.

Constance's cunt was now running freely and the air was pungent with the smell of her copious secretions. A steady slurping sound smacked between her thighs. And a constant series of groans and sighs escaped her lips. She could feel tremors up and down her legs and a deep melting in her belly. Her asshole, sore from the previous fucking, began to yearn for more penetration and she felt herself pushing the anus out, silently pleading to be entered.

She so totally forgot herself that at one point she tried to buck her pelvis forward, to assist the man in his violent treatment of her tender pussy. But she could not move even a quarter of an inch. She was perfectly pinned and could do nothing but let the man have his way with her. She could hear him grunting and cursing and imagined what a sight she made for his hungry eyes. A young beautiful woman completely helpless, her cunt an open prize for his hands and tongue and cock, her tits bound, the nipples tortured by nipple clips. For an instant she was able to identify with him and it caused a ripple of vicarious pleasure to join the sensations she was already feeling. Without having any conscious design in the matter, she slipped suddenly over the brink into orgasm and heard herself shouting as she came.

And above her own noises, she heard the high-pitched maniacal laughter of the man.

"All right, bitch, here it comes," he yelled.

And then pulled his four fingers out and bunched them into a fist and thrust the fist with all his force into the yielding, slick and spongy tissue of her cunt. She cried out with terrible pain. But he did not pause for a split second. The fist exploded inside her. She came to the very edge of passing out, but did not make it into unconsciousness. She hung there for a very long time, not knowing whether she would be able to breathe or not. He did not move. It was a moment of almost unbearable intimacy. He held her at the brink of death, it seemed, and so she was totally dependent on him, had to bear him good will, had to keep him in good spirits. And he was at a point of penetration that very few men ever experience with any woman. And she could not see him.

When the vaginal walls began to recover from the immense trauma and started to relax, they stretched over his fist. The very tiny serrated opening of her cunt was stretched to an obscene width around his wrist. Without wanting it, she made a very tiny adjustment of her pelvis, tilting her cunt up toward him an infinitesimal fraction of an inch.

"OK, baby," the man said. "Now you get it good."

And with those words, he began to move his fist. First he twisted it around, and then he pulled it back an inch and pushed it forward. The sensations Constance felt were indescribable, far and beyond anything she had ever known in her life. It was as though an enormous cock was filling her entire body, going from her cunt to her brain. She swooned with the overwhelmingness of it.

Then he began to punch-fuck her. He pounded his fist into her cervix hard enough to bruise it, but not hard enough to damage it. He drew his fist back until it filled the opening to her pussy, until that tiny hole stretched to its maximum width and left Constance in a profound flurry of surrender, and then crashed forward, the entire fist erupting inside her in a single violent thrust. He punched her again and again, a score of times, a hundred times, a thousand times, until her pussy was punch-drunk with pain and pleasure. At moments it felt as though he was inside her up to his forearm. At other times he seemed to be raging unrestrictedly, his fist twisting and turning inside her.

She was long past the paltry experience known as orgasm. The man was taking her to a place which transcended all definitions. She had become pure, vibrant life, the electricity sizzling up and down her spine, exploding in her brain. Her legs and arms had become antennae sensitive to all the cosmic currents slicing through the illusion of solidity presented by the thing we call matter because our organs of perception are too gross to see the true energy dance beneath the appearance.

It was beyond sex, beyond orgasm, beyond LSD, beyond any mystical experience she had ever known. It was the pure realization of naked life knowing itself as naked life, awesome, mysterious, and eternal.

And at the very peak of that awareness, the man pulled his fist out with brutal abruptness. All at once she became a pit of empty despair, a black hole of infinite emptiness, howling its loneliness to the stars.

"Ooohhhhhhhhh . . ." Constance wailed.

Her cunt was a gaping wound, wide, red, pulsing wildly, like a ravenous, toothless mouth sucking for food, a blind fish's mouth, or an infant's mouth, or the mouth of a very old woman.

"Ooohhhhhhhhhhh . . ." she cried and her mournful cry seemed to reach to the very sky.

"Man oh man, is she busted wide," the man who had been fist-fucking her said.

"Look at that," another man added.

"You could drive a truck through that cunt," a third man chimed in.

"Ohhh," Constance moaned.

"Want something, baby?" the first man sneered.

"Gi . . . gi . . . giv . . . give . . . it . . . to . . . me . . ." she gasped.

"Want my fist? Want my big fist up your juicy cunt?"

Constance was in a decided dilemma. A few hours earlier she had been a normal woman with a normal sex life. Then she had been abducted and drugged, and within a very short time had found herself enjoying being fucked in the ass for the first time in her life, and then being fist-fucked to the point where, suddenly, she knew she would not be able to do without the experience again. She wanted it, and wanted it badly, and wanted it at once. And all her pride rose up at having to admit it to someone who was intent on tormenting her, a sadist who had paid to abuse a bound and blindfolded woman. But she had no choice. The man was waiting for an answer.

"I'm waiting for an answer," the man said as though reading her mind.

"Yes," she said softly.

"Yes what?" he prodded.

"Yes, I want you to shove your big fist up my juicy cunt," she said.

The man chuckled. Constance felt his fingers trailing up and down her crotch, his hot, lewd fingers casually stroking her most intimate parts. The sheer shamelessness of it all brought an unaccustomed blush to her cheeks.

"Let's try this first," he said, and insinuated one finger into her asshole.

Constance sucked her breath in. The sensation was sharp and unexpected, and not without an edge of pleasure around the initial burst of pain. He withdrew it and she felt his hand return to smear a huge glob of warm lubricant between her ass cheeks. He tamped it inside her and then, rudely, shoved three fingers into the puckered hole. The pain was intense and she tried to pull away but she could not budge an inch. Instead, she let out a loud howl of protest. The only reaction to that was mirthless laughter.

"Loosen up, sweetheart," the man said, "because I ain't gonna stop till I got my fist up your pretty little ass. I wanna prove that fags ain't the only people that can do it."

"Oh no," she whispered. "You can't. I can't. You'll kill me. You'll tear me apart."

In response he pulled out his three fingers, giving her a second's respite and then shoved four in. She let out another wild cry, but she noticed that it had a shade more drama than actuality in it for indeed she was loosening up and the insertion of four fingers did not cause noticeably more discomfort than three had a few minutes earlier. He twisted his hand and twirled the fingers around in her asshole. She lay there, bound, open, spread wide for his use, and could do nothing but push down to try to relax the opening to save herself damage, but in the process gave him the pleasure and satisfaction of watching her open to him, and further began to experience no little amount of pleasure herself.

"Oh my God, I'm beginning to enjoy it," she said to herself.

The man pulled his fingers out and paused. She knew what would come next and she hung in the balance between fear and desire. She was terrified at the possibility and yet her heart beat in expectation at such an outrageous act, something she would never have ordinarily even thought of trying.

He slipped the five fingers of his hand, brought together in a point, into her asshole. And he pushed straight in right up to the line of the first knuckle. With someone at liberty to move, he would have had to pace himself, but since Constance was perfectly bound, he could go as quickly as he liked. He pushed further until all his fingers were in up to the second knuckle. Constance was at the breaking point and felt as though he must tear her apart.

"Take a deep breath," he said.

She did, and squeezed her eyes tight. Then, with a single abrupt gesture, he curled his fingers under, balling the entire hand into a fist, and thrusting forward at the same time. In a single fluid movement, he had slipped his entire fist into her asshole.

Her first and overwhelming reaction was one of profound and complete rapture. She had never known anything so absolutely wonderful in her life. It provided a sensation so unique, so fantastic, so far beyond anything she had imagined possible, that she was amazed that everyone wasn't doing it all the time. She wanted to spread her legs even wider but her ropes didn't allow for movement in any direction.

The man divined her feeling however, for he shoved his fist forward. His arm disappeared into her bowels and was swallowed up to the elbow. The asshole allowed of far deeper penetration than the cunt, as many homosexuals have discovered, and Constance was treated to the full opening. The man pulled back until his fist was at the very rim of her asshole, held it there a second and then plunged in again past his forearm.

He fist-fucked her for a half hour until she was giddy and ready to believe that she had died and gone to heaven. All the other considerations of her life disappeared, her name, her age, her work, in short, her entire identity dissolved and merged into the volcanic sensations produced by the action of a man's large fist and arm frothing in and out of her asshole with wild abandon.

And when she thought that nothing more could be imagined or felt, he called another man over.

"Get one in her cunt and we'll fist-fuck her in both holes at the same time."

Constance's soul shuddered, but when the second man began working his way into her cunt, she yielded with surprising ease, and it was less than a minute before he was completely inside her. Then both men went at her with gusto, and practically shook hands through the thin membrane which separate cunt from colon. They shoved their fists into her like a baker kneading dough. Sometimes they alternated and sometimes went in and out together. In the first instance, the ripples were like the wakes of boats passing one another in a lake. In the second instance she felt as though a huge log were being roughly shoved into her belly and sucked out again leaving her wistful and hollow.

There seemed to be no more that could be added on, but just when the extraordinary condition of being simultaneously fist-fucked in cunt and ass by two different men was beginning to lose its novelty, a third man climbed on top of the table and shoved his thick, hard cock into her mouth. The tip was already slimy with pre seminal fluid and her first taste of him was that salty tang. He bore down hard and slid his cock deep into her throat causing her to gag. As she gagged, her cunt convulsed and her asshole tightened, making each of the men at the other end exclaim in wonder.

"Pussy's fighting back," said one.

"Asshole's getting hungry," said the other.

And they redoubled their efforts, punch-fucking her holes until they were once again battered into passivity. But then the man at her head shoved his cock into her throat again, and again she convulsed and tightened involuntarily, and again the other two men beat her physiology into submission. That formed the new pattern, and Constance became a single, raw muscle, an exposed nerve, played on by three men who found their mutual validation by using the woman as conduit for their energies.

"I don't know where I am or what this is about or how it's going to turn out," she said to herself, "but one thing I do know. I'm round the bend. Something inside me has snapped and I'll never be able to go back to anything like a normal sex life, not after experiencing *this!*"

The man at her head finally came, his sperm splashing on her tongue and oozing down her throat. He held his cock there until she had swallowed every drop, and then even longer until she had licked it clean.

"My arm's getting tired," said the man with his fist in her asshole.

"Want to fuck her?" said the first man.

"I want her to suck me off," the second man replied.

He crawled up on the table and slipped his cock into her mouth and held it there.

"I done enough work on you, honey," he said, "now you do some."

"Fair enough," Constance said. "But I can't move my head."

"Use your tongue and suck a lot," he replied.

And that is what she did. While he kept his cock in place, she licked the head over and over again, and clamped her lips over the shaft and sucked and sucked, and did this until he felt the first tremors in his thighs, and the lickings of heat in his balls, and the sweet meltings in his spine. And when he finally spilled his sperm, it pulsed into her mouth and she drank it deliciously, sucking the tube to get every last drop, and then licking him gratefully.

When she finished, the first man, who was still fist-fucking her cunt, said, "That looked good. I think I'll try some of that."

"Oh yes," Constance purred. "Let me have your big fat cock in my mouth." And smiled to herself. She shuddered at what she was about to do, and yet it seemed absolutely logical and necessary that she do it.

He pulled his fist out of her and she shuddered with its disappearance. She felt something of the same pang she did when she had lost her virginity. This was one more "first" she would never be able to experience as a first again. She felt a certain gratitude to the man who had broken her fist-fucking cherry, but she wasn't going to let sentimentality get in the way of irony.

The man put his knees on either side of her head. He slid his cock in between her lips. It was thick and flat and slick with the fluid that had seeped from the tip during all his exertions. She licked the tip clean, and then nibbled at it. He had given her quite an experience so she wanted to return the favor as much as possible.

She sucked his cock for a very long time, using all her patience, strength, and knowledge. He crooned in response.

"Oh yes, baby," he moaned. "That's the way, the way I like it. Suck it, lick it, take my hard cock into your beautiful sweet mouth. Wrap your lips around it. Lick it with your hot tongue."

Constance hummed and sucked, licked and hummed. She could feel him growing closer and closer to orgasm. And she knew that that would be the moment of truth. All her life she had been dissatisfied because she felt that she had never been presented with a chance to prove her true mettle. She'd begun to climb the ladder of success in her profession, but there was little risk or danger. She wanted to be put in a complete crisis situation so she would know whether she was worthy of her own beliefs or not, whether she had the courage of her worldview. She was convinced that to each human being there comes a moment when destiny steps in and demands that he or she do something totally outrageous, totally outside the context of normal behavior.

The man above her began to moan consistently. She knew that he was very close. She licked harder and sucked more strongly. The cock throbbed and pulsed and grew hot in her mouth. It was every cock she had ever sucked and she flung herself into eating it with abandon. She was approaching her own climax, one which would go light years beyond anything she had ever known or imagined. Being fist-fucked in the ass and cunt, being abducted and turned into a slave, these were not mundane occurrences, and the test of her soul would be whether she was truly transformed by them.

The man let out a cry. His back stiffened. The cock popped out of her mouth. She opened her lips wide. His sperm shot all over her face. She curled her tongue up. He plunged his cock back in. The sperm kept shooting. And shooting. And she sucked and sucked until he was completely dry.

Then she put all her strength into her jaw, flexed, brought her teeth together in a single, horrible bite, and severed his cock from his body at the very root.

The man, as predicted, let out a scream, a cry of pain and shock, fell from the table, and was dead within minutes. Constance spit out the member and, after taking a deep breath, swallowed the blood that had spilled into her throat.

"Blood and sperm," she thought, "a fitting combination."

A few more minutes went by and then she sensed someone else standing next to her. She tensed in apprehension.

"Interesting," said a male voice, one which she identified as Smoothy. "But, of course, I warned him. And he, of course, got caught up in his triumph and forgot. Well, no great loss. We have his money and can dispose of his body."

She felt his hands on her breast and realized that he was removing her nipple clips. Then his hands went to her feet.

"But I think we'd better get you out of these ropes," he went on, "before anything else happens. Your extremities are beginning to turn blue, and we wouldn't want you to get gangrene before you've been of full use to us. Especially not since you've proven yourself such a promising victim."

With that, he leaned forward and kissed her on the lips. She thought she detected a trace of affection in the kiss, but thought that that must be pure hallucination.

2

The room was as pleasant a space as any she had ever lived in. It was some twenty feet long by twenty-five feet wide, with a large private bath, and sported a balcony which received continual sunlight. The appointments showed imagination and taste: an oversized double bed with a large mirror for a headboard, a walnut writing desk, a walk-in closet, bureaus, wall-to-wall forest green rug, a very subtle use of lamps to provide modulated lighting, a stereo, a radio, a television. The effect was that of a personalized and expensive hotel room.

Constance didn't know where she was geographically. From her window she could see only the sea. The grounds seemed to be situated at the edge of a cliff; the surrounding terrain was very heavily wooded. After her ordeal she had been taken to her room by Smoothy, who formally introduced himself as Robert, and given a preliminary overview.

"This will be your room for as long as you are with us," he said. "While here, you are assured complete privacy. Later, someone will show you where the kitchen is. Also, we have a swimming pool, exercise courts, a free commissary where you can get beauty aids, sanitary napkins, magazines, newspapers, and so forth. The grounds are perfectly guarded with a combination of electronic devices, trained dogs, and armed guards. Escape, of course, is never, strictly speaking, impossible, but your chances of getting out of here are practically zero."

Robert had delivered this all in a pleasant, lilting tone. He was a man in his late twenties, with soft, wavy brown hair cut medium-long to his shoulders. He was a bit over six feet tall, wispy thin, with a delicate, fey manner of speaking and gesturing. He gave the general impression of taking daily milk baths and having his fingernails buffed. He was dressed in forest green velour pants—a color that dominated the entire establishment—with a pure cotton, dark brown turtleneck shirt. He wore silk slippers. Constance had been naked, bruised, caked with sperm and dried blood, and aching for a hot bath. He had seemed sensitive to her condition and need.

"I know you want to be alone, to clean up and to gather your thoughts, and I'll save the rest of the orientation talk for later. I just needed to let you know this much. I'm sure you'll be bursting with questions after you've cleaned up and had a good night's sleep."

He glanced at his watch.

"Your next shift is at four tomorrow afternoon, so I'll be by in the morning to take you to breakfast and we can talk then. And, by the way, if you need anything, there's a buzzer next to your bed for room service. And a maid will be in each day to make the bed and clean up."

He had smiled with what looked like genuine warmth, cast a quick, appraising look at her body, and then said, "Sleep well, my dear."

Constance flung herself on the bed and shook for five minutes. Up to that moment she had maintained perfect control. When she was tied up, she reasoned that panic would only inflame her tormentors. And after her brief walk to the room when Robert had taken her blindfold off and given her that brief talk, she was too stunned by the rapid change in ambience to do anything but hold tight. Then, as soon as he left, the dam burst and her feelings flooded through her with uncontrolled force. In such a short period of time she had been captured, drugged, fucked in the ass, fist-fucked, and had murdered a man by biting his cock off, and all of it had flowed with a sort of surrealistic ease that threatened to pull away all the pinnings of what she ordinarily considered reality.

She finally finished trembling and staggered into the bathroom where she treated herself to a very long, hot soak, a shampoo, and then brushed her teeth, rinsed her mouth, and brushed out her hair until she had regained some modicum of normal identity. She went into the closet and found a soft linen bathrobe which she put on. On the night table next to the bed she found a pack of Pall Mall, her brand of choice and habit, and a flashy lighter. She lay down, lit up, and sank contentedly into the soft springiness of the mattress.

15

She was into her second cigarette and the beginning of a sense of calm when there was a light tapping on the door. Constance was a woman of high survival instincts, which meant she spent no time on foolish meandering over questions to which she didn't know the answer. Things would be made clear or they wouldn't; meanwhile, the major issue was to center herself, to become one with her new environment.

She thought it was Robert at the door and called out, "Come in," without hesitation. But when the door opened, she was more than a little surprised to find three beautiful women standing there, each scantily dressed. For an instant she feared they might be coming in to "get" her, but their vibes were friendly. She pushed herself up on the bed and smiled.

"Come in," she repeated.

The three women moved in slowly, like cats sniffing out a new territory. Then, seemingly satisfied that the place was safe, they closed the door behind them and fanned out to approach Constance from three sides, to end by sitting in a semicircle around her on the bed.

"Hi," said the one to her right. "I'm Sally." She was a woman of about nineteen, blond hair down to her waist, gently cupped breasts, and a wide, lush mouth.

"Sally Carter, Sioux City, Iowa," Constance said. "Disappeared, May 23."

The woman gasped.

Constance turned to the other two. Madge Campbell, Five Corners, New Mexico, and Sheila Dean, Moon City, Colorado. The first woman was a dark-skinned beauty of Indian extraction. Very short, a lean, hard body with disproportionately large and soft breasts. Sheila was a freckle-faced redhead, seventeen years old, with the abashed look of the perpetual virgin setting her green eyes at complete variance with the dirty-girl body under them, a broad, fleshy, simmering torso with the slight musky odor of randiness always hanging over it.

Constance smiled complaisantly. "I'm a reporter," she said. "I began to learn about the disappearances of young women all around the country. And I wrote an article about it. Maybe that's why I got grabbed. Anyway, I've seen all your pictures and know your stories."

She paused. "My name is Constance, by the way, and I'd like to ask, where the fuck am I and what the fuck's going on?"

The three women started talking all at once, but Constance silenced them and pointed to Madge, who seemed to be the most adult of the group.

"I don't know too much," Madge said. "I got kidnapped and chloroformed and when I woke up, three guys were fucking me at once. I tried to pull out but somebody slapped me and I was injected and put under again. Since then I've been on call about four times a week for the past three weeks. It's about

16

an eight-hour stint, and sometimes it's easy and sometimes you get put through changes that turn your hair grey. And on off-duty hours I can take it easy and pretty much do what I want." She nodded at the other two. "Their stories are about the same."

"Any idea of how long they intend to keep us, or who *they* are?" Constance asked.

The faces of the other three darkened.

"I don't know anyone in the organization except Robert," Madge went on. "And as to how long . . . well, until somebody pays a high enough price to get a girl he can kill, and then they choose one of us and that's the end of it."

Constance felt a knot in her stomach begin to tighten and burn.

"You can't be serious," she said.

"I've already seen one go. A nice kid, too. Name of Wendy. They told her it was her time, and she cried and screamed but they dragged her away, and she's never come back."

"Oh my God," said Constance, the true horror of her condition beginning to sink in. "What can we do?"

"Forget it," Sheila put in. "When you get a chance to walk around, you'll see how impossible it is to even think of getting out. A sheer four-hundred-foot drop in front. A twenty-five-foot wall around the other three sides. And dogs and guards and invisible electronic screens."

"I ran into one of those," said Sally. "I was walking on the other side of the garden and all of a sudden bells started to ring and in about ten seconds I was surrounded by three men with rifles."

"So it's a prison," Constance said.

"And we all have the death sentence," Sally added, and with those words lost her composure and burst into tears.

Madge immediately leaned over and slapped her hard across the face. Constance was stunned by the action. But Sally stopped crying at once.

"It's a pact we've made," Madge explained. "The one thing that will destroy us faster than anything else is self-pity. So if anyone sees it in anyone else, the others are authorized to step in and stop it."

Constance's eyes lit up. The feeling of camaraderie was infectious and she found herself, in this most bleak of all circumstances, smiling broadly.

"I know this is weird," she said, "but I'm really happy to be with you ladies. I read about you and wondered about you, and even though it will probably cost me my neck, it's good to see you and feel the strength you've acquired."

As she spoke, Madge held out a slip of paper which she motioned toward Constance, and at the same time held one finger to her lips. As Constance read the note, Madge said, "Well, since it's hopeless that we'll ever get out of here, the only thing we can do is to keep up our good

17

humor. And, in between sessions, we're treated pretty well. I mean, it could be worse."

The note read: "The room is probably bugged. In a minute I'll suggest that we have an orgy, and once that gets started I can tell you more from behind the moans and groans."

Constance was completely taken aback. The note itself sent a shiver down her spine because, despite the fact that she was in a life-and-death situation anyway, the notion of revolt scared her. But the way in which the orgy had been so casually suggested was equally astounding. Constance had never had relations with a woman in her life. She had never even fantasized about it.

"It's getting warm in here," Madge said in a loud voice. "Do you mind if I take these things off?"

"No, go right ahead," Constance found herself saying. "And you two can make yourselves comfortable too."

The three women shrugged out of their various robes and panties and shorts. Constance held her breath. She had never seen so many naked cunts and bare tits in her life. The sight, however, was not nearly as powerful as the scent. Deep, musky, female, the trapped odors from between their thighs and breasts filled the air and the room became heavy with the smell of womanhood.

Madge winked at her.

"Oh, I'm a little weary," she said in the same stage voice. "Do you mind if I lie down?"

Constance shifted her body a little to one side. She was surprised to notice that she was perspiring lightly. The oddity of the entire situation was now producing a new perspective from within itself. She was not only about to enter into her first lesbian act, but it was to be a foursome, and done as part of a revolutionary movement on the part of women who were plotting to save their lives.

"If I lived to write about this," she thought, "it would make an extraordinary allegory. But the very point of my survival is why I am being drawn into this situation in which I will be licking the secretions from the cunts of three ladies I have known less than fifteen minutes, smelling their assholes, stuffing their tits into my mouth, and having them ream out my pussy with their fingers."

"No, make yourself at home," Constance replied.

Madge lay down next to her, her face near her thighs. She stretched out full, her tiny, lithe form a dark cutlass of flesh on the sheet. Sheila and Sally inched closer, their eyes gleaming. They sat cross-legged and Constance could see the pink slits of their cunts beneath the patches of pubic hair and elephantine outer lips. Unaccountably, her mouth began to water.

"It's a nice thing to do," Madge said in a low voice. "After being brutalized in the Parlor, we come together and remember what it is like to be tender, to be soft. We cleanse ourselves from the imprint of the male flesh with the juices of our female bodies."

As she spoke, she slipped her hand under Constance's robe. The fingers trailed lightly on her skin. She parted her thighs. Her cunt was already gooey with secretions. Madge's fingertips found their mark and ran up and down the slimy slit. Constance shuddered and her buttocks contracted involuntarily.

"I killed a man today," she said.

"Oh?" Sally replied. Her eyes were already clouded over with desire and her body swaying back and forth to some discrete inner rhythm. She leaned forward, both her hands falling on Constance's ankles. Her fingers slid up, curving over her knees, atop her taut thighs, and up to the juncture of leg and torso, that slight indentation which forms the valley, left and right, of which the cunt is the throbbing core. Constance's robe was lifted by Sally's sweeping forearms and she was now naked from the waist down.

"Oh Mommy," Sally crooned and buried her face between Constance's thighs, her tongue slipping out at once and seeking the pungent juices. As Constance watched, Sally worked herself into an autistic frenzy rubbing her face into the rapidly engulfing cunt. She glanced over at Madge who shrugged and lifted her eyebrows and in general indicated that each human being has her own idiosyncrasies and who are we to judge? And, without missing a beat, she leaned forward and covered Constance's mouth with her own.

Constance fell back on the bed, being kissed at upper and lower mouths Sheila, not to be left out, unbuttoned the top of Constance's robe and let her full breasts fall to the sides, then cupped each in one hand, brought them toward the center until the nipples touched, and covered the doubly-sensitive point with her hot mouth, tonguing the already wrinkled disks and their twitching tips with slobbering abandon.

Constance opened her mouth and spread her legs and let herself be had. At this point, it didn't seem too much different than what had taken place earlier. Her bonds were not ropes and chains but the demands of necessity. On one level, everyone born on the planet was a slave, a slave of blind circumstance. The most joyful and exultant feeling possible to a human being is that of realizing that we are indeed one with all creation and that creation is finally and ultimately mysterious to itself. There is no one or nothing outside the totality from which the totality is viewed. And the totality can not know itself except insofar as it differentiates from within. Thus do we come to male and female, life and death. The totality did not choose to be here as it is anymore than any individual awareness within that totality. To exist at all is to be enslaved. The only question of any validity is the comfort of the condition at any given time and place.

These speculations were interrupted by a voice whispering in her ear.

"There must be a way to escape. But our only hope of finding it is to keep pretending that we've lost all hope of finding it."

It was Madge. The words came in between the other woman's sliding her tongue into Constance's ear, so that the message was a collage of heat and meaning, wet and syntax, sex and politics. Sally continued in what was beginning to appear to be an epileptic fit between Constance's thighs while Sheila was sucking the soreness left by the clips from Constance's nipples.

"The only chance we have to exchange messages is when we are pretending to have orgies," Madge went on.

"It's a most realistic pretence," Constance thought, her pelvis twisting and bucking and the first sweet tremblings of orgasm pulsing at the tip of her clit.

Constance turned her head so her mouth was at Madge's ear. "Do you have any hard information for me?" she asked. "How many women are in on the idea? Is there any notion of an escape plan? A route?"

Madge reversed their position. She tapped Sheila on the shoulder indicating that she should make more noise. Sheila obliged by increasing the volume of the slurping she was doing. Sally had already hit a high decibel level in her seeming attempts to lodge her entire head in Constance's vagina.

"All the women have been contacted but we can never all be together at one time, so information is passed in overlapping waves. There's a lot of distortion. We have no plan, only a general readiness. And the only conceivable route is down the face of the cliff. The wall is impossible and even if we got over it, we'd be picked up very quickly in the woods."

"The cliff!" Constance repeated.

"We've said enough," Madge whispered. "You'll have to be here a while to pick up information before you can be really useful. When you have something, contact any woman not on duty and get into an orgy with her and a few others and pass on what you've learned. It will get around to everyone within a few days."

"But . . ." Constance began to say.

Her sentence, however, was cut short by the implantation of Sheila's cunt on her mouth. The woman had tired of working on Constance's breasts without receiving any attention on her own, so she took matters into her own thighs and presented her pussy to Constance's tongue and lips for ministration. Constance was momentarily paralyzed by the sudden presence of a hot, hairy, wet, smelly pie of flesh and membrane pressed over her mouth. She didn't know quite what to do with it, but instruction was not long in coming.

"Suck it, you prissy little bitch," Madge said in a loud voice, reverting to the stage tones with which the orgy had started. "You've had enough cock in your life, let's see how you like one of your own."

"How far must I carry this masquerade?" Constance thought.

"For as long as you live," a voice answered in her mind. "You are trapped here, in this scene, on this planet, in this life. And you have no choice but to act out what's given to you."

"I suppose you're right," she sighed mentally, one part of her personality concluding the dialogue with another. And with that inner surrender, she gave herself up to exploring the common practice of eating cunt, thereby reconnecting herself to her animal nature.

Sheila was young, firm, hot. Her cunt had all the elasticity of the teenager, all of its sense of naughty pleasure. Although she was a member of the woman's liberation movement and so ritually indulged in the orgies in order to pass information, her interest was not in leadership or organization. Madge and a few others had concocted the scheme and kept it alive. Were it left to Sheila or to Sally, the hopelessness of the situation would have allowed them to sink into self-pity, or simple debauchery, or to spend their time in the frivolities of vanity, passing their days in gossip and society.

Madge's words to Constance were a real goad to Sheila and she repeated them, but without the edge of drama.

"Suck it, you prissy little bitch," she said and pushed her weight down even heavier onto Constance's face. Constance had a bit of trouble breathing but once she adjusted her angle so that her nose was clear, her mouth was free to make its own explorations. Her tongue curved up and dug into the juicy little honey pot of the hot-assed, spread-thighed, humping lady above her. It was a brackish fluid that slid down her throat, but the very edge of odiousness was what gave the act its wry tone of eroticism.

Constance opened her mouth wide and stretched her lips as far as they would go, engulfing the pumping snatch and pulling it into the vacuum she created by emptying her lungs through her nostrils. Sheila's cunt lips surged into Constance's mouth. She bit her lower lip as the sensations of blood flooding the tender membranes enflamed her imagination and she slid into a revery of what she had experienced the night before when she had been tied to a slab and had sugar shoved in her cunt and spread in her pubic hair and then had a jar of ants poured on her belly. The insects whirred about in a tizzy of release and danced wildly on Sheila's stretched skin. Then they smelled the sugar and descended on it like a ravenous army. The insects rushed pell-mell into the thatch of hair like soldiers plunging into a wheat field. They pushed on over the outer lips, roamed the inner lips, and finally followed the powdery trail into the very hole of her hole, spread wide by a distender specially engineered for the purpose and locally referred to as "the cunt horn." Sheila had gone mad with screeching delirium as the long trail of ants marched briskly into her pussy and roamed the inner walls at will to reap their harvest. All the while, a number of men had stood around her and laughed uproariously, pausing only to fuck her mouth or her ass or pinch her nipples. Sheila had found the entire episode explosively erotic, the thin line between acute sensation and biologic repugnance providing the most exquisite sensual tension she had ever known.

Now she tried to relive the memory as Constance sucked the juice from her snatch and swallowed with hungry curiosity. She had never admitted it to anyone, but her being kidnapped and thrown into this baroque milieu had rescued her from a life of suffocating ennui. The small town, the idiot boys she dated, with no hope for the future except a dull marriage and a repetition of the patterns her parents had grown grey on. Here she was involved in a nonending series of erotic surprises, maintained a lively social life, kept a diary, which, she flattered herself, showed literary merit, and had formed several deep friendships with other women her age. In addition she enjoyed an erotic freedom with women she could never have known otherwise. It was, for her, ideal, except for the fact that she would one day be killed, but then how was that different from life, in which she would one day die from one cause or another?

She pushed down, forcing her belly down, flexing the inner muscles of her vagina, and filled Constance's mouth with the soft, mucous mounds of the inside of the deepest part of her cunt. Constance was seized by a fierce flurry of gulping, licking loss of control. All the lifetime associations she had with cunt flourished in her consciousness. The piss hole, the gash, the bleeding wound, the stink pit, the sticky slit . . . all the terms and feelings of opprobrium governed the instant of her awareness that she was really lying on her back while a strange woman forced her convulsing cunt into her mouth.

"Mmmmm," she moaned, straining to suck more of it in.

She couldn't see the gesture, but Madge looked up and caught the eyes of the other two women, Sheila looking down and Sally peering up over Constance's pubic hair as her own mouth continued to slice into Constance's pussy, and nodded. The expression indicated, "Good work, now we've got her."

She then moved up with marked rapidity and pushed Sheila off her perch. Constance was stunned, gasping like a harpooned hippopotamus. Her mouth had become a blind leech and would have sucked at anything put against it. Madge knew that, and supplied her own cunt as object. Constance cried out in gratitude and lost herself in the act.

It is a commonly understood but rarely communicated truism of sex that it attains its ultimate point of gratification when the triple barriers of gross, subtle, and unconscious resistance have fallen and a kind of permission is given to the whole person to let go and indulge the moment. Then we drop identity, attachment, and parity, and become pure sound, pure movement, pure life. At such times, the mind bursts its barriers and we sail into the realm of infinite awareness, in which the form becomes utterly inconsequential and we dwell masterfully as mistresses of eternity. Then, to suck a cock, to lap a cunt, to lick an asshole, are of no importance whatsoever, for one might as easily be watching a sunset, pondering a galaxy, or writing a symphony. It was into such a state that Constance gratefully sank. She no longer had to be considered with who or what or how or why or when. No one was expecting any response from her. She was being offered the ultimate erotic pleasure, the gift of being left alone during the act.

The four women then sailed on into the evening, letting the tapestry of their actions be woven by the random promptings of their desire. At one point they had gravitated into a double-couple, Constance on her back, Sheila on top of her, Madge and Sally at either side, also facing in. Their mouths all met, and lips and tongues slid and washed over one another with complete indiscriminate exploration. At the same time, eight hands roamed below and felt four cunts and four assholes, a dance of fingers that had them all squirming like worms in a fishing can.

They impaled themselves on the pinnacles of their own forgetfulness, losing track of time of day and where they were or why they were supposed to be indulging themselves in the first place. Each was lost in a private revery, one now a teenager in the back seat of a car, another a newlywed experiencing the first penetrating bliss, a third a whore causing kingdoms to topple, and the fourth a hitchhiker being raped by a motorcycle gang. They came to their individual and collective conclusion, rested, smoked, and began again. Constance was, among other things, the "new asshole in town," and these were the first three of the women to taste her. Before the month was up she would be had by every woman on the grounds.

At one point Madge got up to go to the bathroom, and Sally put a record on the stereo, while Sheila rummaged in the pocket of her robe and pulled out several joints. The four women then sat in a circle and smoked and listened to African rhythms and moved their asses around on the bed and ran their fingers through their hair and hung glances on one another through smoke-squinting eyes and got old and tough and silently assessed the universe. They were troopers, torn from the fabric of their common lives, thrust into a context of terror and coruscating eroticism, and were now passing the scanty information of escape from the prison by whispering secrets into one another's cunts.

By and by the joints were finished and the music changed to throaty blues and Madge took Constance in her arms and began to make love to her. This wasn't the wild, scattered thrashing of half an hour earlier. This was local, personal, intense. The other two women lay back, side by side, fingering one another's cunts with easy, desultory movements, while Madge cupped Constance's buttocks and pulled her cunt up to be met by her own, and ground her pubic bone into the other's clitoris, and sucked deep kisses from her lips.

Now it was a time of demand. The earlier mode of interdependent tripping was finished, and the emphasis shifted to total dependence. With each thrust, with each caress, with each kiss, with each look, Madge demanded response. The essence of her lovemaking was to rouse the other to respond, to evoke the most thrilling expressions, the most wanton gestures. A dozen times Constance tried to roll over onto her belly so that she would offer her vulnerable buttocks to Madge's control. And the tiny movement was always met by a smile of smirking superiority. This wasn't an exchange in which Madge hoped to give and get, but a military program which she was trying to win. She wanted Constance to surrender, not to her, but to herself. She wanted Constance to display herself, to open herself, to put herself on parade, and then to allow Madge and the others to feast on the garden of sprouted delights.

Madge slid to one side and, licking Constance's breast, brought her right hand between the other woman's thighs.

"Open it, baby," Madge said, "open your luscious cunt to the world."

And when Constance had spread her legs as wide as she could, Madge simply slipped her fist into the wildly dripping hole. There was no pain, no strain. Only a swelling rapturous pleasure, a yielding. Constance lifted her legs high in the air and opened them to the skies while Madge, frowning in gentle concentration, worked her fist in and out with lugubrious ease.

"Oh, let me," Sally breathed.

"Me too," Sheila added.

And one by one the other women took their turns, Madge pulling her slime-coated fist out and each of the others shoving theirs in. Constance did not make a sound or move an inch. She was lost in a cotton-candy revery of pure immediacy. She was lying in a strange room in a horrible prison while three women took turns fist-fucking her and all she could think was that this was the most sublime thing that could ever happen to her and that she never wanted it to end.

And yet it did. Fatigue, the natural cessation of certain rhythms, an orgasmic glut, all combined to push the four ladies back from their endeavor. And, as is often the case at such moments, when they had rested a bit, and smoked a bit, and peed and run combs through their hair and put their robes and various bits of clothing back on, they realized they were hungry.

"Well, let's go down to the kitchen," Sheila said.

"Oh, why bother?" Madge replied. "Let's call room service and have them bring something here."

"It's pretty fancy," Constance said. "Even hotels don't provide meals at all hours of the day."

"Well, it's a twenty-four-hour place," Madge told her. "The johns come in at all times and the sessions go around the clock. When you do your first session without a blindfold you'll see what it's like. Anyway, all the antics make the customers hungry, and at the prices they pay, the establishment wants to keep them well fed."

"It gets like a gambling casino," Sally continued. "And it's like each of the slabs or pieces of equipment is a table. One is a roulette wheel and another a craps table and another black jack. And while each girl belongs to the man or men who paid for her, they almost always let other men have her too. So the men kind of wander around the room, trying to find out where the action is."

"And we're the games," Madge said bitterly. "They hang us up and spread us out and spin us around and whip us and shove things in us and piss on us and we don't mean any more to them than any other toy they use to amuse themselves."

There was a moment's silence.

"Anyway," Madge continued, "that's why the kitchen is always open. And as to room service, well, why look a gift horse in the mouth."

"The menu is in the desk drawer," Sheila said moving over to pick it up and bring it back to the bed.

"I'm a vegetarian," Constance said. "Or, I was, I guess, until I bit that guy's cock off this afternoon."

"Yeah," Madge replied. "We all do something like that at the beginning, but the novelty wears off. Besides, if you do it three times they get really pissed and do you in. After the second one you're given a warning. They usually treat their clientele with as much disdain as they treat us, but they can't allow themselves to get a reputation for this kind of thing."

"I want a steak," Constance said, "rare, with a baked potato and sour cream, and a crisp fresh salad with oil and lemon, and a good red wine, and afterwards coffee and cheesecake." She looked around and smiled. "What the hell, right? The condemned woman ate a hearty meal."

"That's the spirit," Sally said.

"I'll have the same," Madge put in.

"Me too," said each of the others.

Sheila reached over and pushed the buzzer next to the bed.

Ten seconds later, there was a light knocking on the door. The women looked at one another, surprised.

25

"Well, that was fast," Constance said. "You can't complain about the service." And in a louder voice she called out, "Come in."

Robert was standing at the door. Behind him were two men. They had black hoods over their faces.

"Oh my God," Madge said in a voice that made Constance's blood run cold.

Robert stepped inside. His entire manner was one of apology.

"I'm sorry," he said, "but we've had a request . . ."

A short silence spaced the room. Finally, Madge stood up. "Which one?" she asked, and couldn't conceal the tremor in her voice.

"Sally," the man said.

Sally cried out once, then pushed her fist into her mouth and closed her eyes. The other women closed around her and hugged her. There was no movement for a full minute. Then Sally stood up slowly.

"I'm ready," she said.

She walked to the door, turned, smiled at the other women, and then whispered, barely audibly, "Good-bye." Then she walked quickly out of the room.

Robert nodded to the three women, his manner dripping diffidence, and stepped outside, closing the door behind him.

"The bastards," Madge muttered.

A few seconds later there was a second knock. Constance let out a whimper, but Madge walked briskly to the door. When she opened it, a short, slightly stooped man of about fifty stood there. He was dressed in a faded butler's uniform, a peculiar anachronism.

"You rang?" he said in a high-pitched voice.

His words hit the ambience of the room like a mallet striking a gong. It was a very long time before Madge replied, her voice firm.

"Yes," she said. "Steak, rare; baked potato with sour cream; a crisp salad with oil and lemon; a good red wine, and afterwards, coffee and cheesecake."

"And how many will that be for, madame?" he asked.

Madge could not control herself any longer. Tears gushed from her eyes and she turned away. Constance stood up and walked slowly to the door.

"That will be for three," she said.

3

They sat next to a large open window overlooking the sea to have breakfast. Robert was jauntily dressed in cotton slacks, a bodyform T-shirt, tennis shoes, and socks. The entire outfit was a pure white. She had allowed him to escort her to the dining room and order coffee and rolls, freshly squeezed orange juice, and a filet of whitefish which had been caught just an hour earlier. It was an unusual breakfast. But Constance had shown by her attitude and manner that she held Robert in contempt for his part in taking Sally away the night before.

They were into their second cup of coffee and first cigarette of the day before he spoke.

"Your feelings are understandable," he said. "But your behavior unsophisticated. I had imagined that you, more than any of the women we've brought in, would grasp the reality at once and make a complete adjustment without wasting time on bemoaning what can't be helped. It's gauche for me to point it out, but your time is limited, and you have no other viable value but to live as fully as possible while you have the chance."

"I'm well aware of the existential implications of the situation," she replied coolly. "But believe me that my present distaste for your company provides me with as full an emotional complement as I could wish."

"I'm prepared to accept your mood because I find you attractive. You are the oldest woman we have ever had, and so add a touch of much-needed maturity to the available provender. Also, you are perhaps the most intelligent. I read your article, and then dug up earlier things you had written. You might have had a brilliant career if your lust for sensational stories hadn't ended you here."

"So my article was the cause of my kidnapping." Constance crossed her legs and lit another cigarette. She was wearing loose orange slacks and a short-sleeved blouse, and had decided to go without shoes. On the outside she had limited her smoking to three a day, but here she had no hopes for any real longevity and an extra five or ten cigarettes a day would add a pleasing recklessness to her sensibility.

"We reasoned that after your failure to get it published anywhere but the *Enquirer* you would move on to something else, but we couldn't take the chance. You would have come across more stories about disappearances and would probably have gone to the FBI or some such group. Besides, during the week we were watching you, I developed an overpowering curiosity to have you."

"And has it been satisfied sufficiently?" she shot out.

"Oh, I haven't touched you yet. And I won't, until you come to me freely. One of my staff privileges, of course, is my pick of the women, so I could order you for the Parlor or for my private room at any time, but I'll wait."

"What on earth makes you think I'd ever go to you freely?" she said. "After all, you are a murderer."

"Because sooner or later you will grow hungry for a relationship with a man. Something that can't be satisfied on the gaming tables, or by your little lesbian follies. And I *am* intelligent, affable, warm, friendly, and good-looking. And there is another reason, one you ought to have figured out already." He smiled at her, and the gap between the boyish expression on his lips and the deadly calculation in his eyes quite mesmerized her for an instant. "Those who are nice to me get a little check put next to their names, and when a request for a Snuff candidate comes along, those names tend not to get picked." He waited an instant for the full weight of his words to sink in, for her to realize that he had the power of life and death over her. "Also," he added, "I am authorized to take an occasional woman out for a sail, or horseback riding past the walls."

He read her expression with open delight. "Ah, I can see dreams of escape dancing in your brain already."

"And I get special treatment if I fuck you?"

"No, my dear, not fuck. I can get that any time. What I want is total surrender. Real surrender. True exchange. I want you to *like* me, to think about
me, and to look forward to being with me. When you can accomplish that, I
would think that your position here would be very solid indeed."

"And if I don't, then I can look forward to an early demise."

"Oh, you are safe for a couple of months at any rate. It takes that long for
novelty value to wear off. After that, the girls get case-hardened and go
through their paces in the Parlor practically yawning, like old hookers. And
nothing is more displeasing to the type of customer that we get to perceive
that he can inflict the most imaginative horrors imaginable upon a woman and
have them be treated with distraction and ennui. This, of course, drives him
to further excess. And finally, nothing will satisfy him but killing her. And so
our supply is diminished by a process of natural selection. The women evolve
to their doom."

"Tell me something," she said, squinting over her cigarette, "don't you have
any qualms at all?"

"No," he replied breezily. "I long ago decided that the universe was utterly indifferent to everything we here on earth consider among our most
esteemed values. When I was nine I witnessed an earthquake. Bankers and
paupers, priests and prostitutes, good men and vile rogues all fell together.
Since then I have watched death claim its members with total egalitarian
cheerfulness. I know, as much as it is possible for anyone to know anything,
that this life is the only life there is. So I came to the conclusion that I could
do anything I wanted, or could get away with. This position came about, and
I took it, fully aware that I was choosing a life of Absolute Villainy. No, I have
no qualms."

"Are you one of the . . . what shall I call them . . . owners?"

"Hardly," he replied. "I don't even know who they are. I work for a level of
executive below the highest level. And, if I may foresee your next question, I
have been here three years. As far as the age of the place itself, I'm not sure.
Of course, in a sense, it has been in existence from the beginning of time. The
only difference now is that with increased population and intensified wealth
over a larger number of people, the demand for women is greater. But slavers
have been operating for as long as there have been people."

Constance stared out at the sea for a very long time, and before her eyes
the whole of history seemed to sail. Ships and caravans and the movements
of tribes, carrying war and goods and gods and the eternal threat of enslave-
ment, the making of one human being into a piece of property for another.
She saw the vision in all of its ramifications, not only in the relationship
between master and slave itself, but in that of lord and serf, boss and employ-

29

ee, husband and wife, parent and child, church and believer, politician and citizen, rich man and poor man, human and animal. Fleetingly, she thought of Chet and wondered what he would think of her disappearance. Briefly, she considered that he might guess at her kidnapping, and find a way to track her down, but in the face of the power and expertise of the organization that had taken her, anything he did would accomplish little more than to endanger his life. She would never see him again, and her eyes misted over.

"I think I'd like to go back to my room," she said at last.

"Of course," he replied, jumping up to pull her chair away as she stood up. She stepped clear of him, took a step away and then turned to face him.

"I don't know how I'm going to handle it yet," she said. "I may accept the situation in its entirety, with all its ramifications, including the ultimate debasement of falling in love with you. Or I may kill myself. Or I may just let things slide and await my turn. Or I may try to escape."

"Of course," he said, "I wouldn't have expected any less of you, including your honesty in telling me this."

"Well, then . . ." she said.

"Au revoir," he said, bowing slightly.

When she returned to her room, she found a large manila envelope on her desk. Before opening it she undressed, took a shower, and when she was refreshed, sat nude on the balcony, the warm sun kneading her skin, to look at the contents of the bulky envelope.

The first enclosure was a sheet of paper giving her her Parlor schedule for the following three weeks. She had four eight-hour stints each week, some in the afternoons, but most at night, and one beginning at six in the morning.

"Weird," she thought, "any man who would be interested in S&M at that hour."

Under that was a letter officially welcoming her to "The Villa." It read:

Dear Constance,

From one viewpoint, the fact that we have kidnapped you and made you available for violent use by a number of anonymous men puts us in a rather formal and strained relationship. On the other hand, what's done is done, and it is foolish to live in the shadows. You might protest that it is all very well for us to "forgive and forget," because we are in a superior position, but that is true only from a relative viewpoint. On the scale of absolute reality, our petty dramas are beneath insignificance, and what we enjoy or suffer, or how long our lives go on, makes no difference within the space of a century.

Aside from the duty hours assigned to you (which you can look upon simply as a job, and which makes you no different than you were when you lived on the "outside"), you are at complete leisure and liberty to enjoy yourself. All the amenities are here, including a wide variety of media (all the current films are shown in our theater and all our women and staff are encouraged to par-

30

ticipate in our theater group). There are sports, the best medical facilities, a boutique sporting the latest fashions. Under special circumstances you will be allowed to go sailing and horseback riding. About the only things not allowed are telephone calls and incoming mail. If, however, you wish to write to someone to assure him or her of your well-being, we will mail the letter for you (after reading it, of course).

There is the delicate point of The Snuff, and we would be less than honest if we didn't mention it. There is no real justification for our subjecting you to this, except to note that death comes to us all and so we are not tampering with nature but merely making a few minor adjustments in relation to time.

Well, there it is. We are slavers and through one circumstance and another, you happen to have become one of our slaves. If we can accept our mutual destinies, then we can aspire to a modicum of happiness within our common limitations on this planet.

So, enjoy your days and nights, perform your tasks with verve, and make yourself one of the family. We're sure that after a while, what with your work and your off-duty diversions, your love affairs and hobbies, time will pass smoothly and you will come to realize that what happens here is as much life as what happens anywhere, and so make your peace with your condition.

Sincerely,

The Management

When Constance finished the letter, she let it fall to the ground beside her and closed her eyes and remained for a long time without moving, without thoughts, soaking in the rays of the sun. She was calm, resigned, relaxed. Although the fact of it struck her as somewhat peculiar, she was at peace. So many things which provided anxiety in her previous life were missing here. She had no fear of random violence, of unexpected rape or attack. She had no worry about paying the rent. She didn't know where she was geographically, but suspected it was a subtropical climate; she wouldn't have to worry about the cold. Her life had become neat, compact, totally rationalized.

Finally, she poked into the envelope and dug out the rest of the material. It included a map of the grounds, with forbidden areas marked out. There was a brisk description of security measures and a warning about the futility of attempting escape. There were color brochures in which different facilities of the place advertised their services, including the library, the discotheque, the arts-and-crafts shop, the adult education center, the yoga center.

With a sigh, she let the envelope fall to the ground, got up, paced around a bit, and then went back inside where she flung herself onto the bed and without warning burst into hot, copious tears. She cried for a quarter of an hour and then fell asleep.

She had troubled, inchoate dreams and was finally awakened by a hand shaking her shoulder. She looked up. It was the maid, a black girl with cocoa skin dressed in black dress with a white frilly apron, net stockings and glossy pumps. The woman was no older than twenty, wore no makeup, and had hazel eyes.

"Sorry," she said, "but you didn't hear me knocking. It's time for you to go on duty."

"Whaa . . ." Constance said, still fuzzy.

She sat up, rubbed her eyes, and then remembered, remembered where she was and what the woman was talking about. Her heart sank. A taste of cold lead lay on her tongue. Dread tugged at the backs of her eyeballs. Waking up in the middle of the afternoon after a fitful sleep is always traumatic, but to wake up into such a situation, and to feel the first actual impact of it, is indescribable. Constance realized for the first time that her predicament was not an episode but a permanent state, and accepting it intellectually was relatively easy, and even a bit of conceptual fun. But to live it, day by day, hour by hour, endlessly, was something else again.

The maid put her hand in her apron pocket and pulled out a green, cylindrical pill.

"You might want to take this," she whispered. "It'll get you over the worst part."

"What is it?" Constance asked.

"It's got a couple of things in it. Something to give you energy, something to relax your muscles, something to make what's happening feel like a hallucination, something to turn you on just a taste."

Despite herself, Constance opened her eyes in appreciation of the description.

"Oh, it's a nice one," the maid said.

"Why are you being nice to me?" Constance asked.

"I work here," she said. "I like things to be as pleasant as possible. It's part of the policy of the management. And maybe you'll want to do something for me someday."

"What could I do for you?" Constance said.

"Some day, when you have a full day off, we might take one of these together and . . . play."

"Never something for nothing, is there?" Constance said, shaking her head.

"First law of the cosmos," the woman replied. "And I don't make the laws, I just obey them."

Constance smiled and sniffed and stood up and stretched.

"All right," she said, "let me have the happy pill. And one day you come by and we'll get it on. Why the fuck not?"

"Yeah," the woman grinned. "You gettin' the idea."

Constance took the pill, plopped it on her tongue, and washed it down with a glass of water from the bathroom sink.

"How long?" she asked.

"You got twenty minutes to get to the dressing room. The pill will start to come on in about thirty. By that time they should just be bringing you in. They'll tell you what to expect this time." The woman looked at Constance's body appraisingly. "For now, just put on a robe and slippers, brush your teeth if you want to, and comb your hair, and I'll take you to the place."

Constance watched herself in front of the mirror as she did her elementary toilette. Five feet seven, black hair which fell down between her shoulder blades, green eyes, narrow but very full lips, breasts each the size of a small cantaloupe, and a thick, curly bush of oddly coarse pubic hair . . . all combined to make her a compellingly erotically beautiful woman. But far and beyond all these features, it was the swell of her high, broad, and deeply curved buttocks which caused men to turn and stare wherever she went. Her ass transcended the ordinary category and had to be ranked as a *primary* sex characteristic. The number of men who had wined, dined, and covered her with presents in order to place their hands, tongues and cocks into the tantalizing crevice numbered well over a hundred. The number that succeeded were a twentieth of that. And prior to the previous afternoon, only one had fucked her there, and then most unsuccessfully.

She became aware that she was standing there staring at herself in a trance by a knock on the bathroom door. It was the maid. Constance walked out and tittered when she saw the other woman

"You look ridiculous in that outfit," she said. "What is your name, anyway?"

"Carla," the woman said.

Constance was entranced by the glow of saliva on the other woman's front teeth. She leaned forward and brought her mouth close to the maid's. Carla smiled. Constance licked Carla's teeth with her tongue, and when their lips met her knees went soft and a numb hot wet tingling invaded her entire body. She moaned, and melted into Carla's face. She became one flesh with the other woman and for a long time they remained glued to each other, barely moving, except for tiny, quick, exquisite motions of their tongue tips and great breathy swallowings of one another's saliva.

Then Carla stepped back and the whole earth seemed to totter.

"My, my," she said. "We *are* going to have a good time one day."

"The drug . . ." Constance whispered.

"Came on a bit faster with you than with most," Carla agreed and then went to the phone. She picked it up, dialed three digits, and after a pause said, "Bring a chair."

33

Constance sat down and waited, watching herself and the world turn to rubber. The door opened and it seemed to stretch for yards. Robert walked in pushing a wheelchair. He and Carla helped Constance up, slipped a robe over her shoulders, and put her in the chair. And so she went to her assignment, drugged, sensate, wide open, rolling down the surrealistic hallway in a wheelchair.

They brought her to the dressing room where she was slipped into a hood that covered her whole head and left her mouth exposed, black boots and gloves.

"Is that all?" she heard Robert ask.

"It's one of those *nouveau riche* publishers of tit books," the dressing room attendant said. "Made a fortune in less than ten years but doesn't have the imagination to match his newfound wealth. To him this is kinky and far out."

"What's he down for?" Robert asked looking at a clipboard.

"Basic stuff. Three types of whip, nipple clips, fist-fucking, ass fucking, oversized dildoes, suspension from a hanging bar. He wants to finish by pissing on her and coming in her mouth."

"Has he been warned about the rubber bafflers if he sticks his cock in her mouth? She's already bitten one off, you know."

"Yeah, he's been told. Says he's going to jerk off on her."

Constance heard the dialogue and almost swooned. It was inconceivable that they were discussing these things as actual events which were going to take place, and be done to her, as though they were mechanics discussing the performance of a car. But that was merely the beginning.

"How long's he down for?" asked Robert.

"Two and a half hours," the attendant replied. "Then she gets a half hour rest and washing down. And then she goes to Henry for five hours."

"Henry!" Robert exclaimed, in a voice that made Constance shudder.

"Look," the attendant replied, "I only facilitate the orders. I don't make the schedules."

"I know," Robert said. "I'm sorry. I didn't mean to take it out on you."

"Poor kid," Carla muttered.

"She's tough," Robert said, "she'll be all right."

Constance wanted to ask what Henry did but before she could open her mouth, the wheelchair lurched and she was pushed into the Parlor. The din was overpowering. Men shouting, women screaming, a cacophony of harsh breaths and grunts and curses and laughter. The smell of tobacco and marijuana and alcohol was triumphant. There was hardly any air left at all. She heard whips cracking, chains creaking, strange machinery operating. And occasionally, a high piercing cry of a woman yelling, "No, NO!" at the top of her lungs. The chair stopped moving and she heard a low cackle next to her right ear.

"Here she is, Mr. Caccione," the attendant said. "Here's your checklist. Please look it over and sign it. If you subject her to any unauthorized abuse, we reserve the right to name the size of the penalty payment."

"Yeah, yeah," the voice said. "Gimme, I'll sign. Then lemme have her, gimme that luscious pussy. Oh man, look at that bush, look at them tits. Oh, I'm gonna fuck her good. I'm gonna give it to her good."

"Also," the slightly pedantic voice of the attendant went on, "If you wish to have her used by anyone else, he must keep within the limits of your checklist, and each such use will be added as an extra on your bill."

"Sure, sure, money's no object," the voice said. "Hey, Irwin, com'ere," he shouted. "Have a piece on me."

Constance was pulled up, pushed back until her buttocks hit a cold leather slab, and then her arms and legs were tied down. The slab was tilted until it attained the horizontal, and for the second time in two days, she was blindfolded, drugged, and tied down on her back while some strange man prepared to do vile and disgusting things to her.

"I wonder whether understanding him compassionately would help me to accept what he's doing?" Constance thought as the man ran hot nervous fingers over her flesh and slobbered on her breasts. Her thoughts were like distant clouds, for the drug had succeeded in dissociating her from her sense of self. She was a slave to sensation. The pulsing of her heart, the circulation of her blood, the breathing of her skin, became the screen upon which all else took place, and those processes were so impersonal she could hardly claim them at all. She had difficulty telling the difference between her body and that of the man who was debauching her. The whip fell on her like summer rain, and his fingers in her cunt were like the tongues of kittens on the eyelids. She swallowed his fist as easily as she would a bite of ripe pear. The nipple clips seemed as soft as the mouth of a toothless infant at her breast.

At one point, when the man had called several others over, and Constance was allowing herself to be totally consumed by the attention she was receiving, the entire activity suddenly took on a clinical, biophysical cast. Fist-fucking transmogrified to a grotesque anatomical idiocy in which someone found pleasure in mucking about in her entrails. Her insight at that instant struck at the heart of eroticism, which is that it does not exist except as an image. The straightforward need which sends pole into hole, or tongue into mucous membrane, or mouth onto flesh stick, is a function of hydraulics. A certain tension builds and is discharged. But when the discharge is not allowed, for one reason or another, the tension, amplified by distortions of muscular armor, erupts into phantasmagoria. Since there can be no satisfaction at that level, the person is driven to imagining wilder and wilder acts, and unless this process is harmonized, can drive the organism into bizarre behavior, which is then rationalized and synthesized within a context of consensual validity, otherwise known as subculture. Thus, for a man to slip his fist in and out of someone's asshole is not an *act* in the ordinary sense of the word, but a *meta-act* in which image confronts the outer limits of physical tolerance.

"What's going on here is nothing more than an *idea*," Constance realized, and in a stroke liberated herself from eroticism entirely.

Having done so, she was free to appreciate the actual details of what was taking place. The pain in her nipples was just right, sending delicious zigzags of electricity through her. The suspension by her wrists from a hanging bar was perfect for pulling all the excess tension from her limbs and torso. The whip was an intermittent arousal from her tendency to fall into occluded revery. The fists in her ass and cunt provided the perfect non-attainable goal of insatiable fulfillment.

The experience was given rococo overtones by the raucous din all around her, and by the awareness that the men were as unreal to her from her point of view as she was to them from theirs, and wondered if they had the simple intelligence to realize that.

"If they did," she reasoned, "the war between the genders would be instantly transformed by a fiat of abstraction into something like a chess game. Then we might contend with gusto."

It occurred to her that she might not have attained to that insight unless she had been hurled into this extraordinary situation, and inwardly smiled at the irony by which slavery became the fulcrum for elevating freedom.

"Unfortunately, it's a message I won't survive to deliver," she thought, "and if I did there would be no way to communicate it. What would I say, 'I attained my enlightenment while being fist-fucked in a slave parlor'?"

Her ruminations were cut short by an abrupt reversal of posture. She was pulled down from the bar, flung on the table, and tied once more. It was time for the oversized dildoes and the finale. It was impossible for her to tell how big the shafts were that were shoved inside her, but they felt at least the width of fists. Again, it was the old one-two, into the cunt and into the asshole. She was already learning how to make certain inner adjustments in order to accommodate an act, which, she was certain, had archetypal roots.

Spread-legged, nipples pinched, orifices stuffed, helpless, she felt fingers pry her mouth open and rubber bafflers stuck in place between her teeth. With her boots and gloves and hood, she offered the classic picture of bondage.

The warm spicy liquid came next, splashing on her belly, on her breasts, on her pubic hair, and then trailing up her torso, like a tubular waterfall on her chin, and finally into her open mouth, spraying her tongue and collecting in a pool at the back of her throat. He pissed until it seemed there could be no more, and still it kept coming. Then she realized that it was splashing in several places at once, and that there must be four or five men standing over her, pissing on her. There came a moment when she could no longer keep from swallowing, and, as much as the blocks between her teeth allowed, she gulped, the briny fluid slushing down her throat.

"She swallowed it!" one of the men shouted.

"Hooray!" the others shouted.

And amidst their cheers and applause, she lay in perfect shame until they had finished turning her into a living urinal.

True to his word, the one who had bought her then straddled her head, and masturbated gleefully until he had spat his sperm also into her mouth. Then he quickly slipped the bafflers out, forced her mouth closed, and held her chin until she had gulped and swallowed his spunk.

"Whew!" she heard him say.

She was untied, lifted up, put back into the wheelchair, and whisked into an anteroom. There, a man she had not seen before took off her mask, and other apparatus, picked her up, dropped her in a tub of hot water. Two women appeared who then washed her down. She was rinsed, dried, and combed. She was given a mouthwash and told to brush her teeth. Someone handed her a glass of warm milk with honey. She drank it and felt her strength returning. The drug was wearing off but she was still surrealized by its aftereffects and by the impact of what she had just been through. She was pushed into a chair, and one of the women stood in front of her and carefully applied lipstick to her mouth. Then she was slipped into a pure white, transparent negligee. The man came over and before she could react, slipped a hypodermic into her arm.

"Not to worry," he said, "it will only paralyze your vocal cords and jaw muscles. Henry gets embarrassed if the woman speaks to him at all."

"Why not use a gag?" she said even as she felt her throat beginning to constrict.

"Then he wouldn't be able to kiss you," the attendant said. And smiling, added, "You'll see."

Henry was a massively wealthy man whose weight kept stride with his bank account. Well over three hundred pounds, he presented that perfectly bland and benign facade behind which fat people hide. He had the desperately reassuring manner of a nervous dentist.

He had rented a private room off the Parlor, and Constance was led in and tied to a rather plush leather table. The difference was that it was double width, and while her left leg and arm were fastened to the sides of the table, the right leg and arm were manacled to the center. When the attendant left,

Henry took off his clothes and climbed on the table, his flesh rolling and jiggling. Even that minor exertion had him perspiring and breathing hard. Constance looked at him with undisguised distaste, but instantly she realized that that was precisely what he wanted to inspire. There could be few aphrodisiacs more powerful to an insecure man than to have a beautiful woman, who is tied down and at his mercy, disgusted by what he intends to do to her.

"Oh shit," she thought, "this is going to be unpleasant."

He kissed her for over two hours, pressing, insisting, insinuating. He licked her lips, thrust his tongue into her throat. He sucked on her mouth and spit on her tongue. He drooled into her. She would have bitten off his tongue if she could.

His moans and sighs and grunts were as repulsive as his actions. His enjoyment was gluttonous, regressive, beyond simple self-indulgence. He gloried in the degree to which he could impose himself on her.

His basic scenario seemed to be, from what she could glean from his mutterings and exclamations, that of teenage virgin and college football star necking on the couch. Her passivity signified the trembling fear of the young girl giving in to her most forbidden, secret, and luscious desires. He not only had her, but he was simultaneously bragging about his conquest to the other players on the team. He was fucking her in public. He was bringing the proud and pristine pussy to its metaphoric knees. Then he was giving her to his friends, watching her gang-banged. He was sullying purity itself and so revenging himself on the God that disappointed him by not existing.

Fatigue finally overtook him and he rolled over and lay there for several minutes. Then he got up, and drew a bottle out of one of the pockets of his coat. It was whiskey. He began sipping at it and smoking a cigar. He frowned and flung himself into an armchair. He started addressing imaginary enemies.

"They laugh at me, they pinch their noses with their fingers when I pass by. Rotten cunts. But I'll show them. I'll buy them all. I'll make them beg."

The tears of self-pity followed the anger, and within a half hour he was ready to visit his girlfriend again. During this time Constance had been able to piece together a fairly cohesive, if basic, psychological profile of the man, although she wryly admitted to herself that it would do her no good whatsoever, seeing as how she couldn't move or talk.

With his renewed ardor, Henry's kisses became unusually prolonged and passionate. Constance now had to contend with the stench of cigar and booze as well as Henry's ordinarily oppressive manner. She imagined that the teenager was at the point of allowing greater liberties, for Henry's hands began to slide down her chest and finally cupped her breasts. He let out an anguished cry and for the next half hour rode the transports of rapture which that relatively simple touch inspired.

38

"If he weren't so dangerous, he'd be harmless," Constance thought.

The conclusion came further down as he finally allowed his hand to cup her cunt and one finger to slip into the moist slit. In grand style, he shoved the entire pudgy middle finger into her and finger-fucked her with a fine frenzy for almost an hour, all the while kissing her madly.

"If he weren't such a distorted little creep, he'd be a great lover."

He balled himself into a knot of sexual tension, working harder and harder, sluicing the secretion-logged digit in and out of her juicing cunt with an energetic abandon. Constance found herself responding simply on the level of pure heat, the movement creating so much friction that she wondered whether her clit might burst into flames and Henry's fancy frothing write a new chapter on survival techniques for the Boy-and-Girl Scouts Manual.

He wrapped his legs around one of her thighs and rubbed himself on her vigorously, the rocking of his pelvis beating in counterpoint to the dancing of his finger and the swimming of his mouth and tongue.

His orgasm was frightening. The stupendous fear, guilt, and horror hiding behind the mountain of fat and the brutal tendencies and the infantile behavior, exploded as the sluggish gobs of thick sperm oozed from his half-erect cock.

Crushing remorse speared him at the very instant after orgasm.

He rose to his knees. His gorge rose.

Constance was sure it wasn't intentional, but when he vomited, his mouth was directly above hers, and since her jaw was paralyzed, she couldn't close it.

"This is too much," she said to herself as she squeezed her brain tight and forced herself to become unconscious. And yet, as she went under, the hot, flaky mass cascading over her face like thick communion wafers in a heavy sauce, her last thought was, "Poor man. He's going to hate himself even more after this."

39

4

It was a week before Chet began to be concerned. Constance often disappeared for several days when she was on a story and didn't always remember to let him know where she was going. But seven days was longer than he was comfortable with. Finally, he went to her apartment and let himself in with the spare key which he promised to use only with her permission or in emergencies. She had wanted him to have access to her place, but also wanted him to respect her privacy.

He let himself into the flat, half fearing he might find a partially decomposed body. Instead, the place looked normal. And that was the trouble. It didn't have the neat look of a place that had been tidied up by someone who was going to be gone for a week. Rather, there was the same casual dishevelled air it would if Constance had just run out for a container of milk. The bed was unmade, the lights on, and when he went into the kitchen he heard the hum of the radio. It had overheated and blown a tube, but was still switched on. He turned it off and gazed around. Bread, now moldy, sat on the table. An opened bottle of beer, now warm and flat, stood next to it.

Chet sat down heavily, his elbows suddenly weak. There was no doubt in his mind. Constance had been snatched. And it could only be due to her work on the story of the disappearing women.

"The Slavers!" he said out loud, and a cold thrill ran down his spine.

He knew it was a meaningless gesture, but he called the police and reported her absence. He said nothing about his idea. It would only confuse the issue and to no point. Also, he didn't want to get involved in such a public way. He reasoned that if anyone could help, it would be the FBI. He resolved to gather all the data he had put together for Constance on the disappearances and, if she did not return within a week, bring it to the bureau.

The police came, poked around, wrote steadily in their notebooks, and left. Chet was free to roam around the apartment. He knew there would be nothing by way of a clue, yet he felt he should search anyway. It took him two hours to look through Constance's clothing, books, papers, toilet articles. The only thing of any interest was a packet of love letters written to a man she had been having an affair with years earlier. He couldn't resist the temptation to read some, and when he had, he wished he hadn't.

"Do you know what you did to me last night?" one read in part. "When you plunged your donkey cock into my cunt and I tore the skin off your back with my nails, I died a thousand times. Worlds were born and died. I wanted to swallow you whole. I gave myself to you completely and eternally. And no matter what I shall ever feel with any other man, he will never have me as you did. Never, I swear it."

He snickered and smirked but part of him was hurt. It also made him think back to his early loves, when each woman shone painfully bright in her uniqueness and each love was the birth of a new reality. And while he understood, conceptually, that everyone who loves feels the same, yet his heart kept whispering that this was the first time in the history of the world that precisely such a love had been known. Then there had come the so-called sexual revolution, when one did not speak of a woman but of a cunt, and love was considered an antiquated euphemism for fucking. Chet had fucked his brains out, almost literally, until he had attained the ideal of the brief epoch that defined the late 1960s: he was no longer able to tell one woman from another. When he met Constance, he was trying to recapture the earlier innocence, knowing that that was impossible.

"Yet," he had reasoned, "if I live according to the way I used to feel, perhaps I will get some of my belief back."

It hadn't occurred to him that Constance had a parallel evolution. And as he looked down at the picture of her on her dresser, he wondered if he really knew her at all.

41

"What is it?" he thought, "three years? How little time that is in relation to one's entire life. It's less than a tenth for me. When I match her against my parents, my old friends, ex-lovers that I still maintain a relationship with; when I match her against *myself*, then she's practically a stranger. I've met a handful of her friends. I don't know her former lovers. I've never seen her parents. I know nothing of her childhood except a few superficial facts."

Chet was forced by her disappearance to look with unusually honest examination into just what it was that existed between the two of them. And it dawned on him that he was not relating so much to her as to his relationship to her. That is, he was involved more in the structure of what they did together than in her herself and in herself. There had been flashes from time to time when he was able to distance himself and view her as though she were a stranger, but even that was a theatrical gimmick and partook more of the superstructure than of the actual contact.

Ultimately, he found, that sex with her had ceased to be an erotic act as such, for it lost the necessary tension of surrender to the forbidden. In return for the loss of the erotic mood, he received good, healthy, pleasurable fucking. It was obvious that eroticism was an ego function, having to do with conquest, mastery, show, and questions of curiosity and novelty. A cunt is a cunt but to slip one's fingers into a cunt one has not known before contains a basic appeal that no amount of pious intentions regarding the bond with one's beloved can obviate.

Yet, she represented certain values that he felt he had to incorporate, although even there it was uncertain as to whether they were nothing more than reflections of an essential insecurity concerning his vision of existence. He was, in fact, afraid to come to a conclusion concerning the nature of things for that would have implied a decision about how he would live his life, the subsequent betrayal of which would have rendered him radically impotent. It was better to pretend not to know, and accept the essential paradox of relationship which makes us progressively uninteresting to one another the more real we become. For, beyond illusion, which is distance, only self-reflective unity exists. He was faced with the conflict between the comforts of eternity and the poignant beauty of mortality.

He tidied up the apartment, put out the lights, and locked the place behind him as he left. Each phase of his departure was etched in hyperrealistic awareness, for the ritual was suffused with a searing sense of finality. Perhaps Constance was dead. He realized that he was not overly upset at the idea. He only felt the turmoil of his emotions when he thought on how she might have died.

"Or she might be installed in a harem somewhere," he said to himself and found himself smiling at the image of Constance dressed as Lana Turner and leading palace intrigues with susceptible eunuchs.

It was necessary for him to get laid, that much he knew. Whatever Constance's fate, whatever he decided to do about finding her, the night could not pass without relief. He took a taxi to Forty-second Street and Eighth Avenue, and plunged into the world of dark, callous eroticism. He did not know precisely what he wanted, but understood that under the circumstances the best approach would be to pay for it. That was tactically the cleanest form of exchange at the moment, and, for all he knew then, the only honest basis upon which a sexual exchange might take place.

"What do you get out of it?" a woman once asked after he had fucked her for four hours and taken her to exotic realms.

"The pleasure of knowing that I can do it to you," he had replied spontaneously and then been amazed at his own answer.

"It seems like pretty thin gruel to sustain you for all that exertion," she noted.

This night he wanted no pretences. He wanted to buy flesh because only in that way could he control what went on. It was his gratification he was interested in, not Constance's at this point, and he was struck by seeing that he bore her no little resentment for what he called creeping entropy in their relationship, even though the responsibility for softheadedness was just as much his. He was tired of making love to a person, he wanted to fuck a thing.

The street caught at him as he stepped out of the cab. It was a raw spring night, the smell of the new season an elusive scent beneath the heavy curtain of engine exhaust. No climactic, meteorological, or seasonal nuances survived the city with any significant success. The sky threatened rain, but the sky was an invisible presence behind the midtown glare reflected on the unnaturally low ceiling of inversion.

He walked to Forty-sixth Street and then down to Broadway, savoring the subtle shifts in ambience that occurred each block as the neighborhood went from sleazy to pretentious to gaudy. The side streets boasted the legitimate theatres, fossils still capable of stirring their bones, while the Great White Way was a slash of movie houses, cut-rate junk shops, dingy restaurants, and traffic. When he turned up Forty-second Street again, going west, the very air became charged with soft violence. The dozen or fifteen movie theatres showed hard-core porn or obscure adventure films, kung fu melodramas or new-wave black gangster thrillers. The block held sporting goods stores, which prominently displayed knives, a shooting gallery and amusement parlor, quick-food shops, which made the Broadway restaurants seem centers of high cuisine by comparison, and a moiling stream of drunks, deadbeats, pimps, hustlers, hookers, and boy prostitutes. It was an avenue of pure tawdry experience, and Chet walked through the scene as though he were in a museum.

Back on Eighth Avenue, the ambience shifted downward into a serious business. Chet eyed twenty or thirty women, mostly black, mostly ugly and scarred, mostly tending toward bulkiness. One caught his attention and he veered toward her. She might have been nineteen or twenty, tall and thin, with an outrageously high and lean ass. She wore a skirt that came almost to her crotch, and a red sweater that outlined pear-sized breasts. Her face was round and her lips full and soft. She was highly appealing and Chet was already picturing her bent over a hotel room bed, the dark crevice of her buttocks opening onto a moist pink cunt.

But when he was several feet away, he stopped. She looked at him with the way that street whores have, a mixture of defense and invitation, a hint that what the man thinks he's buying and what she's selling are probably two different things, and the faint prospect of her actually, in the heat of the embrace, giving herself to him in some dimensional manner. At the very corner of her mouth there was a small, open sore, no larger than a fly, but unmistakably oozing. It could have been a fever blister that just broke, an innocent infection, or the mark of some virulent venereal disease. He teetered for an instant on the brink of asking her outright, but the sheer shamefulness of the entire situation suddenly stripped him of momentum, and he turned abruptly and walked away.

The whore looked after him for a few seconds. Her feet hurt, she had a toothache, and the four men she'd had that evening were all somewhat repulsive. The chance at a good-looking young man had come as a small but real flutter of pleasure, and his brusque flight was felt as a personal rejection.

Chet flagged down another cab and rode to the Village. For someone in his mood, it was definitely not a place to hunt for women. He was impatient, pugnaciously introspective, and horny, and all three traits did not recommend a man to the ordinary female of that area for whom a certain sophisticated pacing was an essential ingredient of the transaction preceding their taking their clothes off and wailing with guttural abandon on the slippery cock of some grunting stranger. Yet, the Village suited another aspect of his mood, for it provided a perfect cruising ground both in the homosexual and nautical senses of the term. It was possible to float through the streets and swim in the stares of those who were on similar errands of ambiguity. Each eye contact was its own form of erotic exchange which did not have to lead anywhere. The glances were like salvos hurled from soul to soul, and one could return fire, or withhold it, surrender, or sail in for the kill.

He found himself drawn down Christopher Street, that sluice of gay eroticism down which are swept the mincing, strutting, shuffling, and simply walking random population of the homosexual world. Dressed in Levi's, leathers, or elegant rags, they provide a unique current of energy, which manifests a buoyancy in sharp contrast to the usual sluggish movements of the city's millions. It is the closest thing to a tribal consciousness visibly available to a casual observer.

Chet was a closet queen. His homosexual encounters were known to no one, not even his therapist. He preferred it that way; it wasn't a question of guilt. The appeal of the scene was less in the act itself than in the absolute privacy, forbiddenness, and squalor of its context. He thought that people who preached gay liberation were stark raving mad. The idea of a *sanctioned* homosexuality seemed to exhibit the essence of the banal sensibility. What more flaccid, hairy, angular, foolish, and distasteful scene could one imagine than the sight of two men in a licit and legal sixty-nine? The demythification of sex through the upsurge of organizations and magazines and movies had already gone a long way toward destroying the fires of eroticism in the land. If homosexuality fell from its privileged perch and became the common property of the masses, there would be almost nothing left for a man of discretion to amuse himself with.

Chet stopped first at Ty's, once a quiet and top-notch leather bar, but since its discovery by the action parasites it had quadrupled its clientele and been reduced to a tenth of its former quality. Now, as a result of the homosexual equivalent of bussing, a kind of subcultural miscegenation had set in and a degenerate breed had been born. Wall flowers with imitation leather jackets wearing the latest coded handkerchief-and-key-ring signals were piled like a day's catch of clams onto the barroom floor, all waiting for someone to brush up against them and provide the first foetid flowering of the evening.

He had three beers, stayed long enough to let the music and vibrations settle into his bones, and having effected something of a transition from his straight identity by this brief run through the sheep dip, headed west to the bookstore.

With curtains on the windows and no sign to explain what happened inside, it was a pit stop for most of the men who cruised the area. The front was a medium-sized space devoted mostly to magazines and a few books. There was also a long glass counter displaying dildoes, vibrators, lubricants, inhalers, handcuffs, and assorted paraphernalia. If one knew the proper way to ask, one could buy poppers from the clerk who kept them in a refrigerator under the counter.

It was the back of the store, however, which provided its true raison d'etre. There, a truncated labyrinth wound about, dimly lit, with twenty-five-cent booths showing short film clips of men having sex flanking the aisle. The booths had sliding doors and were large enough to accommodate two and sometimes three men, depending on their positions. The most intricate arrangement Chet had seen had one man with his back against a wall fucking another man standing in front of him while a third man knelt sucking the cock of the man being fucked.

When there was a goodly number and the heat reached a certain level, quite often the booths were disdained and the antics took place in open view. When Chet went through the swinging doors, his eyes narrowed to adjust to the gloom. It took a few seconds to begin to make out the loungers leaning against the wall, the sperm vultures eyeing crotches hungrily, the impresarios, prima donnas, the one-screw studs, the swooners, and all the types and archetypes of the homoerotic night.

He didn't know quite what he wanted. His cock was tingling and his chest tight. Dropping to his knees and swinging on a lusty joint was often a cure for that kind of malaise. He prowled for a while. He saw one promising bulge but when his eyes skated up the sloping belly, past the chest and into the eyes of the owner, he saw pointed indifference. He moved on. A group of four or five men were clustered around a booth and Chet edged his way into it in order to watch the last minute of a man's masturbating into the waiting mouth of a teenage boy whose eyes were closed in dramatic rapture and who seemed to be yearning less for the cock or the sperm than for the approbation of the audience that had gathered to watch his performance.

Suddenly, the place seemed pointless, and he turned abruptly and strode out, slowing down in the front section to look at the current crop of magazines. Aside from the standard issues showing sucking, fucking, threesomes, bondage, blacks, teenagers, men with unusually large cocks, there was a rash of publications specializing in piss. Photo after photo showed one man or another getting pissed on, and some showed swallowing and gulping. A favorite theme was that of a man being fucked by one man while being pissed on by another. The piss theme permeated all the other classic scenarios, so that there were teenagers pissing and blacks pissing and men with unusually large cocks pissing, pissing and bondage, pissing and threesomes, pissing and fucking, and of course, pissing and sucking.

"Piss is unquestionably *in*," Chet said to himself as he put the last of the magazines down and strode out of the store, the idle gaze of the clerk frisking his thighs as he went.

He walked north and west, going up Greenwich Street past the warehouse section where the trucks were parked, huge vans and trailers like steer in a pen ranged over parking lots near the Hudson River. While he didn't go in to any of the enclosures, he had been there often enough to know that hundreds of men were at that moment performing a wide variety of sexual acts in the deserted spaces. On warm nights during the summer, the deserted back of a trailer might contain forty or fifty men in a single orgiastic heap. He idly reflected that on all the occasions he had sucked cocks in the dark or licked assholes in anonymous groups, he had never worried about venereal disease. And yet the merest possibility of it had warned him violently away from the

46

prostitute. It seemed as though it ought to have provided an insight into the difference in his attitudes toward men and women, but he was not inclined to pursue it. The years he spent attempting to analyze and understand just what homosexuality was, what heterosexuality was, appeared as fanciful time-wasting. One did what one did and made one's peace with it. And if finding peace required attaining psychiatric approval, then that was all right too. But so much nonsense had been written and spoken over the simple act of putting a penis into one's mouth that he couldn't bear to add to the weight of the stupidity, even if he kept it in the realm of thought.

He finally arrived at The Chorus, a bar that was in imminent danger of being discovered by *New York Magazine* and the *Village Voice*, thus becoming a watering hole for the hordes of mediocre people who gain their information by having it spoon-fed by publications that serve no purpose but to keep air in the bubble of their own hype. As yet, its only contamination arrived in the form of chauffeured and bronzed, ruthless men with slender women wearing white gowns slit up the side. The wealthy, slumming.

The place had a show, which was the cause of its beginning to attract wide attention in the straight world. Chet walked in twenty minutes before it was scheduled to begin. He had to piss, and smiled as he made his way to the urinal. In this milieu, emptying one's bladder was an act of extraordinary complexity, entailing a field of psychoerotic implications.

There were five johns, and the doors were variously painted with large, gaudy letters. The first read, "Definitely Not." The second, "Can be convinced," the third, "Perhaps," the fourth, "?," and the fifth, "Ready!." He went into the door with the question mark on it, that form of ambiguity suiting his mood best. Once inside the water closet, he turned to latch the door, but another question mark was drawn in over the lock. He appreciated the subtlety of the touch and left the door unlocked.

He had pissed and was washing his hands when the door opened and a large man walked in, two inches taller than Chet and much broader. He wore a Modified Truck Driver Outfit in Soiled Denim, the pants deliciously outfitted with genuine grease stains. The accessories were *de rigueur*, key ring hanging from the left side of the belt, a peaked leather cap, a fistful of coarse black chest hair struggling to free itself from the front of the partially unbuttoned flannel shirt. The man made no more than a split second's eye contact with Chet, smiled, and slid the latch over, shutting the two of them in.

He wasted no time on dialogue but began running his hands over Chet's ass at once. Chet's knees weakened, his arms grew heavy, and his lids closed. The man pulled his own zipper down and then opened the belt of Chet's pants and slid the pants down until they dropped from his fingers and fell into two piles around Chet's ankles. From the right pocket of his denim jacket the man produced a small tube of K-Y jelly, squeezed some out, and lubricated Chet's asshole. He put it back, fastidiously wiped his fingers on a piece of tissue, and leaned his weight forward.

Chet felt the erection slipping between his thighs and he opened his legs a bit to give the stranger more room. The man grabbed his cock with his right hand, prised Chet's buttocks open by inserting his left hand into the cleft and spreading his fingers, and brought the blunt tip to the greased hole.

The entry was slow and smooth, Chet relaxing and pushing back as he was penetrated. It happened in a single stroke so that the opening movement of the fuck rose like a sustained chord which swells from the barely audible sweep of the string instruments to the full vibrating blast of the entire orchestra complete with booming bass drums bracketing the harmonic din. They rose together until Chet's buttocks were nestled into the cloth-covered crotch of the man behind him and they were both standing on their toes.

The second movement was longer. A series of short, explosive thrusts which had Chet gasping for breath and bending as far forward as he could at the conclusion of the bursts. The man was holding his hip bones, and had his own knees bent so that his fucks came from below at the perfect angle to invade Chet's colon straight on. In this section, Chet's breath was forced from him and he sounded like a man in the last laps of a long distance race. The stranger sucked his breath in sharply between his teeth.

The third movement was timeless, that is to say, free-form. The man swayed and lunged, paused and humped, lunged hard and gentle. Chet pushed back or remained passive, he squeezed or went lax, he twitched his buttocks or used his hands to pull them apart. They fucked with precision abandon, making no sound except an occasional, involuntary gasp, and their movements wild within the bounds of the discipline imposed by the nature of the environment.

The final movement was classic. Chet hung in perfect balance while the man behind him started a slow, steady climb to orgasm, his penetrations beginning long and easy and gradually transforming into staccato ripples. Halfway through, however, Chet heard a familiar snapping sound and his heart skipped a beat. Even before the ampule was put in front of his nose, he could smell the sweet fumes. The man sniffed first, then held the broken yellow cylinder for Chet to inhale from. Within seconds the effect took hold, and Chet sailed into a storm cloud of intimate euphoria. Universes solved themselves in his mind, his chest was warm with yearning, and the cock in his ass was the primal manifestation of the godhead itself, sending almost unassimilable sensations throughout his entire body.

48

As the man came, spurting rhythmically inside him, Chet opened his lids halfway and looked at his face in the mirror. It was a mask of profound drugged debauchery, a study in instant dissipation, a portrait of wanton existentialism.

After a polite pause, the man pulled out. He caught Chet's eyes in the mirror, winked, and smiled. Then he zipped himself up, bending the still turgid cock to fit inside his tight jeans, slid the latch back, and walked out into the crowd.

Chet stood there for a full minute, his legs trembling. He stared at himself in the mirror, watching himself come down, to return from the previous phantasmagoric flight to the world of consensual gestures, postures, perceptions, reactions. The fuck had been ideal, and Chet was left without a trace. His bowels felt empty and wanted to be filled, and if Chet followed his inclination he could easily get fucked twenty more times. But, if experience were any guide, as he would, after the third or fourth man, get caught in the web of probability, and end with a bell curve distribution of quality in relation to his fucks. The one just finished would almost certainly be among the top two or three, but then he had all the mediocre and unpleasant experiences to look forward to in addition. He decided to pull in the reins. He squeezed the sphincter muscles half a dozen times and pulled himself back together. He gathered up his pants and tied his belt. He ran a comb through his hair, and then turned to leave.

Just as he went to open the door someone pulled it from the outside. He found himself looking into the eyes of a heavy-set man of about forty dressed in well-worn leather. He looked like a serious practitioner, someone who was a master long before sadomasochism had become trendy. Chet nodded to the man and stepped to one side. But just then, he wondered why someone like that would be going into the Question-Mark Room. The man caught his expression.

"It's the only one empty," he said. "And I just want to piss. You know? Nothing fancy."

Chet smiled and went out into the smoke and noise. The show was beginning. There were two major acts. The first was fist-fucking. And that was relatively straightforward. Two men came on stage, one dressed in stereotype leather, the other in only a loin cloth. They went through a rather brief and stiff pantomime indicating a pick-up and follow-through. The mime ended with the second man taking his loin cloth off, with a great show of coyness, and to the accompaniment of whistles and catcalls from the audience. He then knelt on a low table, his right side to the crowd.

The other man reached behind the table and picked up a can of Crisco shortening. The crowd yelled and applauded. He opened it, scooped out a gob of the white grease, and smeared it forcefully between the first man's buttocks. It was impossible to tell whether they had been warming up offstage or whether the passive partner was always ready, but there was no preparation, no introducing of fingers as a preliminary. The man in leather quite easily and dramatically shoved his clenched fist into the submissive's asshole. The arm disappeared clear up to the elbow. He then worked it for about five minutes, twisting, pumping, grinding. Near the end of the time limit, both of them began to simulate orgasm, breathing hard, letting out cries and gasps, until they both "came." The fist and arm were removed, and both stood up to face the audience and take bows. The cheering was loud and general. The actors had more animation in their eyes during this short moment of recognition than they had during the entire outrageous act.

The second act was a solo. A man walked on stage dressed also in a loin cloth. He smiled, bowed to the crowd, and pulled out a box from behind the table. He dipped into the same can of Crisco and greased himself liberally. Then he removed a number of implements from the box, various outsized dildoes, nipple clips, and the usual paraphernalia of the scene. For the next fifteen minutes, he abused himself, punishing his flesh, his nipples, his upright bearing. The various dildoes were sat on, one after the other, until he had anally ingested a tube a foot and a half long and seemingly as wide as a fire hydrant. This drew assorted "oohs" and "aahs" from the men watching.

For the conclusion of the act, he picked up a four-foot cast-iron chain, the links of which were three inches long and two inches wide. For this he required an assistant, and a thin, snippy faggot dressed in modish corduroys strode haughtily onstage.

"Fist-fuck *him!*" a raucous voice rang out, and was met with alcoholic laughter. The faggot flared his nostrils and sent a fine spray of corrosive vitriol in a single fan-glance directed in the vicinity of the voice.

He then picked up the chain and began stuffing it into the bowels of the man now lying face down on the table. It was a prodigious feat, and the last two feet of penetration were greeted by an awed silence from the usually boisterous crowd. The faggot's forehead was beaded with perspiration as he worked with surgical skill to insert the last inch but one of the chain. And when it was all in, he straightened up and paused.

The other man got off the table and walked five steps and then knelt down. The kinaesthetic empathy for what he must be experiencing was palpable and flowed from the pit to the stage. The performer had begun to assume mythic proportions. He then knelt down, his forehead on the floor, his hands pulling his buttocks apart.

The faggot approached him. He seemed slightly grey from nervousness. He bent down and linked the middle finger of his right hand into the portion of the last, exposed link. Then, taking a deep breath, he straighted up, and ran

50

at astonishing speed toward the far end of the stage. The chain sang out like a fishline off a reel when a big fish takes the hook. The links and interstices flew out at an alarming rate, the anus fluttering madly. When the entire chain was out, the far end fell to the floor with a resounding clank. Chet estimated that the thing must weigh thirty pounds.

The man fell face forward and lay on the floor for several seconds quivering from head to toe. He was visibly moved and the theatrical demonstration glided momentarily into the privacy of an unguarded moment. The members of the audience became voyeurs, and an uneasy vibration oozed through the crowd.

But then the man stiffened, came to his knees, stood up, and turned to face the people. He smiled and bowed. And with that, the accumulated tension broke and they showered him with a thunderous ovation. The applause and cheers went on for over a minute.

The man, now a star, nodded to the faggot who picked up the chain, curled it, and carried it into the wings. It was clear that he served, offstage as well as on, as the chain man's slave.

Chet ordered a beer and stood sipping it as the crowd returned to its ordinary anarchic state, having been temporarily galvanized into an army of appreciation by the performances. He felt refreshed and cleansed. He wondered at the acts he had seen, and knew that one could do a doctoral dissertation on the meaning of it all. One saw the end of a civilization, the birth of a new liberty, theater, psychological dynamics, and a host of other categories of definition. Chet had always been amused by the academic naivety of Americans who, upon discovering something, always assume that it hadn't existed before. All the so-called novelties of the sexual revolution offered such shock value to a society only because most people have been hypnotized into accepting official descriptions of reality as the reality itself. When the current period of breaking out came to its cyclical end, the civilization would go back into the closet, and millions upon millions of people will imagine that homosexuality, orgies, swinging, and "perversions" have disappeared. And then be outraged again when the next cycle of exposure arrives.

However, fist-fucking was something else. Chet wondered whether this might not be a historical first. The Babylonians had orgies, and the Greeks had little boys, and the Romans had a glut of various excesses, but he couldn't recall any reference ever being made to fist-fucking. When was the first person fist-fucked? How did it come about? Was it a voluntary or a forced act? When was the term coined? Does the term exist in other languages? Chet, whose girlfriend, he still imagined, had yet to be fucked in the ass, and who couldn't imagine himself taking a fist, was suddenly taken by a lively curiosity about the subject. He had one friend who was a fervid practitioner. And since he had begun being fist-fucked several years earlier, his health improved, his complexion became glowing, and his mental alertness went up several notches. He spoke of it as a supreme yogic exercise and grew eloquent in almost religious praise of its virtues. He once described an experience to Chet in which he had taken mescaline, and while peaking and watching the color-explosion sequence in 2001, he inhaled poppers and got fist-fucked.

"What more could there be?" he had asked.

The thoughts having peripherally brought Constance to his consciousness, Chet tried to focus his awareness on the problem of her kidnapping. It was difficult to compute, because she might already be dead, in which case he felt the best thing to do would be to forget. If she was alive, he knew he ought to try to find her. Fleetingly, he had a fantasy of using the computer to plot the place and time of the next disappearance, catch the Slavers in the act, and follow them to their lair, there to rescue Constance from her captors. But she could be anywhere. The Middle East, India, Africa, South America, in a dungeon of a Southern California mansion.

He thought again of the FBI, and decided that that would be his best chance. If she didn't return within a week, he would take her published story, the printout of the program he had worked out to help her, and any other facts at his disposal, to the bureau and see if they could do anything.

Meanwhile, from across the room, he could feel the stare of a thin, very effeminate boy who wore a velour Fauntleroy suit, three-inch heels, nail polish, eye shadow, and had a button on his jacket that read, "I Am a Sewer."

Chet smiled at him and waited to see what would happen next.

52

5

"Fist-fuck, fist-fuck, fist-fuck!" Madge exploded. "Is that the only thing anyone's interested in anymore! I swear, if I get fist-fucked one more time, I'll scream!"

She paced up and down on the deck that had been built some thirty feet back from the shoreline. It was a day of stunning, silent majesty and beauty. Not a cloud marred the sun's dominion in the sky. Not a flirtation of a breeze teased the mind from its perfect equilibrium. Constance lay naked on the wooden stage and let the sound of the surf, the rays of the sun, the occasional rustle of a bird in the shrubbery, blend with equal phenomenological dispassion into the ground against which her total and vibrant sense of well-being provided the figure.

It was the third day of a long break, and she didn't have to report to the Parlor until five on the following evening. It was now almost six weeks since she had been snatched up and taken to what she had come to refer to as "The Resort," and on particularly exasperating days as "The Last Resort." She had lost five pounds, regained an athletic vigor, put on a tan that would have been the envy of women paying a hundred dollars a day at an exclusive hotel, and developed a keen sense of irony.

"And now that goddamned high-rise," Madge went on, her tirade gathering steam. "It's going to ruin the view, create jams, and pollute the water."

"I should think you would have more serious concerns," drawled Sheila who had taken one of those qualitative leaps in studied maturity common to teenagers. She had dyed her hair jet black and cut it to within a half inch of her scalp. It was utterly incongruous with her complexion, eye color, and freckles, and yet freakish enough to compel attention. With that she had shaved her pubic hair off and now lay, spread-legged, her cunt facing the sun, to soak the heat into her exposed center.

"That's serious enough," Madge replied. "After all, I do have to live here, and I don't see why I have to put up with that sort of ugliness." She paced a few seconds and then whirled to face the two women. "Have you seen the plans?" she asked. "It looks like a Holiday Inn. Square, made out of glass and chrome."

"I wonder where we are," Constance said softly. "I mean, geographically."

"There was a woman here who knew how to read the stars," Sheila said. "She figured we were halfway down the eastern coast of South America."

"What country would that be?" Constance asked.

"I don't know," Sheila replied. "I never was very good at geography."

Their voices hung on the still air, disembodied, distant, soothing. Sheila had visited Constance the night before carrying two of the pills that Constance had been given by the maid on her very first excursion. The maid had never returned to claim her night of drugged passion, and her disappearance was not marked by any special curiosity.

The pills were an extraordinary experience. Without the tension aroused by being propelled into the Parlor, Constance could allow herself to surrender completely to its power. For six or seven hours she had wallowed in the licentious and voluptuous promptings of profound muscular relaxation. She lost her conceptual focus entirely, and entered a state of mild, continuous hallucinogenic dispersion. She became a raw mouth, an exposed nerve, a bundle of sensations without category. She was capable of sliding into extended physiological revery, and at one juncture glued her mouth to Sheila's asshole for nearly an hour, and licked and sucked and swirled her tongue around with aimless abandon.

"We're probably in some cockamamie dictatorship," Madge sang out, waving her arms. She was having such a good time ranting that the two other women found her no intrusion on their mood whatsoever. Constance basked in the deep tingling of her bowels. Sheila had inserted one end of a double-dildo into her ass and the other end into her own cunt and fucked her for what seemed like hours. In the joyful presence of the day's steady heat and the memories of such a night, a swarm of hornets stinging her all over would barely disturb her.

"The way I figure it," Madge said, "is that this place is run by a group of international financiers. They are protected by the military of the United States, and possibly by the CIA. This country is probably one of the ones owned by U.S. interests. I would bet we're on a private ranch belonging to one of the oil families."

At this, Sheila opened her eyes.

The only oil family who owns pieces of South America are the R—s," she said. "And I can't believe that even people like that would run the risk of operating a place like this."

"Why not?" Madge said. "They start wars, they finance fascists who torture and imprison their own people, they play fast and loose with the money market and don't give a fuck that millions go hungry or lead impoverished lives because of their greed for power. What makes you think people like that would stop short of outright slavery? For them, that would be a step in the direction of honesty."

"But what difference does it make?" Constance said, drawn into the discussion at last. "The rulers have been the same throughout history. They're the same in Russia as in America, the same in Iceland as in Australia. They were no different in ancient Egypt. You think there's any difference between the pyramids and the World Trade Center buildings? They're both monuments to a man's pride. Who cares if it's the R—s or not? We're still slaves."

"Ah, the voice of the quietist liberal," Madge sneered, and flung herself down onto one of the deck chairs and lit a cigarette. She smoked in silence and the three women lapsed back into lassitude.

The long curved beach described a widened horseshoe perhaps three miles from tip to tip. Their enclave was right in the center, where the ground rose precipitously to form a high and forbidding cliff. The three women, by agreeing to triple-team one of the stewards, had won the relatively rare privilege of being taken down to the beach itself instead of having to content themselves with the swimming pool in the compound. They had been escorted out of a gate in the wall that surrounded their prison and led down a gently sloping trail to a point on the beach a mile away from the spot directly below the compound. That section of beach was fenced in on three sides and patrolled by guards and dogs. It held a sunning platform and a small bar where they could order drinks and sandwiches.

The steward was, it seemed, of the same rank as Robert, and notorious for his exploitation of the women. For the beach privilege, he demanded the following scenario. That one of the women get fucked from behind by his Great Dane while going down on another woman, and while a third woman sucked his cock. The three of them drew straws for roles and Constance got the dog, Madge got to be eaten, and Sheila had to give the man head.

55

Constance had never been fucked by a dog before and examined her prejudices in the matter. As with most erotic taboos, it was mostly a matter of unexamined repugnance based on an image rather than the reality. What, really, was wrong with the experience? At worst it might prove mildly unpleasant; at best, highly exciting. It didn't seem possible that she could get pregnant, and if she did, she was sure the offspring would constitute a marvel of genetic surrealism.

When the time came, she fingered herself for a while until her cunt was moist, then got on her knees, dropped her face to the floor, and offered her exposed rump. Madge guided the dog to her, patting it and stroking its cock. When the beast was aroused, she lifted its front paws and placed them on Constance's back. Then she slipped the bony tool into the soft, slushy pouch.

The dog began humping at once. Constance was amazed to find her loins flush with heat. She lifted her ass higher.

"This dog's a good fuck," she thought, as the Dane pumped wildly into her.

She felt the first drops of the animal's drooling on her neck as Madge slid under her and offered her cunt to Constance's lips and tongue. Constance slipped her mouth onto the furry gash and began the licking and sucking and kissing and biting which remains unchanged in each human being from the first moment at the mother's nipple, the only difference being in the object which is put in the mouth and the imagery accompanying the act.

Meanwhile, Sheila gobbled on the steward's cock, giving him all the slurping, gobbling, gagging, and dribbling that his pornographic heart desired. She let him feast his eyes on her bobbing buttocks and allowed him to slip three fingers into her cunt and slosh around, knowing that his real interest was in the discrepancy between his actualized ennui and the intimacy of the behavior, that difference of heat and involvement lying at the core of degradation.

It was a relatively innocuous session, used, as they were, to the rigors of the Parlor, and for it they purchased a day at the beach. Once there, however, they discovered that if they went down on the guards who patrolled the area, they might be sneaked onto the strip again without express permission from the steward. The guards were paid mercenaries and as such had no erotic privileges. Thus, when they were descended upon by a trio of oozing women for whom sucking cock, getting ass-fucked, fist-fucked, and gang-banged was considered mere foreplay, they were ready to bend the rules a bit to show the ladies a bit of a good time.

"Let's go in the water," Madge said after stubbing out her cigarette.

"Must we?" Sheila complained.

"We can talk there," Madge told her.

The three women stood up slowly and, stretching the laziness from their muscles, walked toward the water. There were barely any waves, merely one-inch ripples, which fell like exhausted waifs upon the sand. As they went forward, two guards moved out from the brush and came to stand in the sunlight, just far enough to let the women know they were there and holding high-powered rifles. The men had semi-erections as they watched the undulating forms, the jiggling, shifting asses, the swaying tits, the primeval cunts.

The women swam out until they were some thirty feet from shore and then hung there, floating and treading water.

"Do you think they'll bring in a construction crew for the new building?" Constance asked in a whisper.

"They'll have to," Madge replied. "But I'm willing to bet that for the duration they keep us hidden away. Even in a situation they control entirely, they can't afford to let anyone on the outside know what's going on here."

"What's the building for?" Sheila asked.

"Expansion," Madge told her. "They're getting more girls and more customers. They want to offer more services. And I think they're reaching a point where they're developing a bureaucracy to take care of all the details . . . schedules, supplies, salaries, and the rest of it. Richard told me that the building would have indoor squash courts, a fully equipped fourteen-bed hospital, and a reading room with newspapers from all over the world flown in daily."

"What's it have to do with us?" Sheila asked her.

"If they're bringing in a regular construction crew, the site is going to have to have rope. And that becomes our objective. To get five hundred feet of rope. With that, we can go down the face of the cliff."

"Is that all?" Sheila said, squinting against the sun as she lay on her back buoyed by the salt water. "I thought you were going to come up with something real."

"You have any better plans?" Madge exploded, her voice rising.

"Shhh," Constance warned. "No point in letting *them* know what we're talking about.

"It's silly," Sheila went on. "First of all, stealing that much rope will be practically impossible, especially since they will probably be keeping us indoors. Secondly, even if we can negotiate the cliff face, then what? We'll be on the beach, in the middle of the night, in a country where the army and police are run by our captors, and probably fifty miles of dense jungle away from the nearest town of any size. This you call a plan?"

"Oooh," Madge exploded in exasperation and pushed Sheila's head down until her face was two feet under water, her arms and legs thrashing. Finally, she let the other woman up. Sheila was coughing and gasping, water running out of her nose.

"You cunt!" she spat out.

"Takes one to know one," Madge said and began swimming calmly toward shore, her buttocks winking above the water as she moved.

"What do you think?" Sheila asked Constance after a few seconds.

"Personally, I don't want to try anything until I find something that feels absolutely foolproof. I think the worst thing we can do is to get caught trying to escape. We'd never get a second chance. The rope idea seems absurd. Your objections are absolutely correct."

"Do you think she's going to try anyway?"

"Probably," Constance replied. "And, who knows, maybe she'll make it."

They took a few more minutes to enjoy the cool clear water, and then joined Madge on the shore. They decided to go back to the compound, and were escorted by the guards to the gate in the wall. Before being allowed to go inside, however, they had to play French Roulette with the four guards. The women were made to kneel on the ground, side by side, very close together. Then they had to suck off each of the men, one at a time. Each sucked for a minute, and on signal, had to transfer the cock in her mouth to the mouth of the woman next to her. The man came at random, and spasmed his jism into the throat of whichever of the women was riding his joint at the moment. As it fell out, Sheila got to swallow all four orgasms, something which made the other two women a bit peevish, for by the time they were on the third man, they had begun to get into the spirit of the thing and had started to ride their own waves of excitement.

It was like a tableau from the Meat Rack outside of Cherry Grove, as three naked women squirmed on their knees, fingering their pussies more often than not, blindly sucking the cocks that were slipped between their lips. The guards, all men in their early twenties, tall, with hard, taut muscles, looked down at the ladies through lidded eyes and reveled in the juiciness of the condition. Slavery, nudity, and surrender to the abasement of the moment provided blazing aphrodisiacal flashes.

As they were going through the gate, one of the men slipped his hand between Sheila's thighs and cupped her cunt with his fingers.

"Free tomorrow night?" he whispered.

"Yes," she said.

"Meet me here, eight o'clock," he told her, and his invitation was one of exclusivity and romance. As she went into the compound, she was already thinking about what she would wear and the perfume she would put on.

Back in her room, with the rest of the day to herself, Constance was at loose ends. After a bath, she dressed in a short, flared skirt, disdaining undies, and a loose, short-sleeved cotton blouse through which the outline of her breasts and the dark of her nipples were tantalizingly visible. It was the kind of mood which, several months earlier, would have had her out on the street, "shopping," which is the female equivalent of cruising. She would have roamed the department stores and boutiques, stopped for a drink at a sidewalk cafe in the mid-50s, strolled through Central Park, and in general spread her spoor far and wide, reveling in the glances and stares, the impact of the psychic depth charges that men set off between her buttocks as she passed. She would have flirted with the possibility of taking on any one of the hundreds of available fuckers and lovers who would have dropped whatever they were doing to step off with a lovely lady and slide a throbbing cock into hot, juicy, and hungry flesh.

And finally, she would have gone to Chet's apartment, would have roused him from his cybernetic stupor and sucked him into the world of sensual reality. He would have squirmed and cajoled and smiled to himself and run through his entire inner soap-opera of antifeminine notions and then, with a cry, would have surrendered to her heat and lost himself in a quivering dance to the tune of her needling desire.

But here, what with her stint in the Parlor three or four days a week, plus the erotic gratuities given to the guards and the steward, plus dalliances with Sheila and some of the other women, the notion of going on a walk of titillation seemed a much of a muchness.

"And yet," she mused, "too soon do we lie cold in the final fuckless sleep."

She decided to make a tour of the facilities, to check out some of the things she'd been hearing about. Also, she did need to do some shopping and Sheila had told her that the shopping arcade was stocked with the finest items one could find anywhere, a veritable Neiman Marcus of a center. She put on a pair of pumps and stepped out into the hallway, already falling into an unconscious swish of the hips, a small but deadly twitch of the buttocks as she moved. She was very sexy and she knew it. What surprised her, however, was to learn that she was also quite randy.

"Hell is an eternal itch," she thought. "And Heaven is a scratching in just that spot where one's own hand won't quite reach, or, reaching, doesn't really do the trick."

She gave herself one last look in the mirror. She had never looked better. The only flaws on her body were a small bruise near her left eye where an overenthusiastic client had slapped her with a closed fist, and several dozen pink stripes down her back, the result of a concentrated whipping four nights earlier. Each woman was looked over by an attendant while in the Parlor to see to it that no man extract more than he paid for. Also, except for a Snuff, the house policy called for "nothing more than cosmetic damage while inflicting pain of any sort." Thus, the women were protected from having their fingernails pulled out, their hair torn out by the roots, their bones broken, their eyes gouged, their skin severely cut or burned. Thus, a man might hold the tip of a burning cigarette a sixteenth of an inch away from a woman's ass flesh until the hair was singed and the skin pierced with an excruciating pain. But he was not allowed to grind the cigarette out in her skin. He could shove his cock into her unlubricated asshole and make her faint with the searing sudden shock, but he couldn't slip a splintered baseball bat into her cunt. On those rare occasions when a man did get carried away, he was immediately pounced on and dragged off.

This puzzled Constance. If Madge's theory was correct, then all the men who came were part of the same club, nabobs of international finance, and one wouldn't imagine that they would do each other violence over something so paltry as a slave woman's life or looks. On the other hand, if the place were a money-making organization, like a gambling casino, and the men simply jaded millionaires paying astronomical fees in order to do dirty on the faces and bodies and spirits of captive women, one would expect a much more spartan setup without all the niceties to which the women were treated. "They would just keep us in a dungeon," she thought. No, there was something else going on, something she had only begun to sniff out. The instincts of the investigative reporter began to function once more now that the total personality had more or less accustomed itself to the dislocation of context shift. She made a note to begin taking mental notes, and realized that it was more important to her to find out what was going on beneath the surface appearances than to attempt to break out. She had no doubt but that she would have no trouble escaping once she understood the nature of the prison.

She went out into the hot afternoon. It was a typical day on the compound. Twenty or thirty women lolled about, shopping, strolling, chatting, taking coffee in the outdoor café, which was decorated to look like a Paris bistro. The others, she knew, were either on duty, or in their rooms, or partaking of one of the indoor activities. Several guards sat or stood on the rooftops of a few of the strategic buildings, commanding an eagle's view of the entire area. Several of the attendants, a steward, and a man whose position she didn't know but who seemed rather important, were walking toward the single gate, which opened out of the inner compound to the recreation area which ringed it. She imagined they were going to examine the construction site. There were no clients in evidence, of course, the men who came to the Parlor being brought in by a secret entrance, billeted in a totally quarantined building, and allowed to see nothing of the establishment except their rooms, the orgy hall, and the tunnel in between.

She spent several hours making purchases, a delight since no money was required. She had had the tendency, as all the women had, to "buy" more than she needed at first, but when her tendency to glut had fulfilled itself within the first week, she picked up items with an eye to elegant necessity. She had a shopping bag full of things by the time she finished, ranging from food to be kept in the small refrigerator in her room to lipstick to be worn on nights when she needed to remind herself of a previous identity.

She sat at one of the circular tables, under an umbrella, and ordered a Pernod. She kicked off her shoes and rubbed her feet together, sighing with relief as she sipped the cool drink and let herself relax into the mood of the moment. It was bizarre. She might actually be in Paris, or on Central Park South, or in Mexico City. She might actually have done all the things she just did. She might actually be filled with the same feelings, the pleasant fatigue, the vague sadness which always accompanied the dying afternoon, the tenuous erotic tingling which made her legs feel as though they had been massaged for an hour and were leaden with laconic desire, wanting only to fall open and be invaded by a large, powerful, sensitive and tender force.

She had almost made up her mind to go back to her room to masturbate when the voice intruded on her solitude.

"You seem so vulnerable with all your innermost thoughts dancing across your face like sheets blowing on a line, the sun drying them, the wind furling them, and about, below, above, the brainy blue sky, the long green grass, the white slatboard farmhouse in Maine."

The imagery, so familiar yet so removed, captured her vagrant attention and she turned her head to look for its source. A young man, perhaps no more than twenty, sat to her side. He had gleaming black hair, which sprouted in a profusion of thick curls over his entire head, eyes that opened a vista into his soul . . . dark, moist, overgrown with sparkling moss, like the stone walls of a deep well. He resembled nothing so much as a cherub, except that he was suntanned. His torso gave evidence of thousands of hours of swimming and tennis. He was naked from the waist up. His legs, although covered with loose white cotton pants, were obviously muscled and shapely. He wore no shoes. On the table in front of him lay a sketch pad, and his hand, even as he spoke, was tidying up the last few lines of the rapid impression he had taken of her. Glancing even from where she was, and seeing the thing upside down, she knew he had caught her essential beauty and not lost any of the anatomical precision of her face.

"Poetry *and* drawing," she drawled after regaining her composure. "My, my, you must have been sent to the best schools."

She had not intended the sarcasm and hostility, but once it was out she felt the rightness of it. There was no way of telling who the young man was, but it was clear that he was no ordinary personage in the hierarchy of the place. The odds were terrific that he had the power to have her taken off and tied down and left for his pleasure, and she more than suspected that he must be

61

connected to the real owners of the Parlor. He had that fine air of great wealth, which suffuses one from birth. He was a person who never had to do anything other than precisely what he wished to do. Which meant he would be utterly charming and affable, and yet capable of unspeakable cruelty.

He was looking at her steadily, with hard-edged amusement.

"Am I supposed to wait upon your leisure?" she asked, "or can I just get on with my business?"

He smiled, and her blood ran cold.

"I think I'll take you with me for a few hours," he said.

He raised one hand, snapped his fingers, and at once two guards ran out of concealment.

"Handcuff her," the young man said, "the wrists behind the back."

Constance was pulled off her chair, yanked roughly to her feet, and the cold steel manacled her hands together. Within five seconds she was standing in front of the young man, helpless, trembling. This was not a client with an attendant nearby, or even a guard with his own skin to protect. This was a powerful stranger who combined the sensitivity and cruelty of a Gestapo colonel as played by Dirk Bogarde. The man waved his hand and the guards disappeared. A number of the people still in the square looked on with attitudes ranging from idle curiosity to compassion to twitching hunger to see what would happen.

The man stood up. He left the pad on the table. He walked behind her. She tried not to follow him with her eyes. His hand went abruptly under her skirt, finding there only the naked flesh. She pressed her buttocks together, but his fingers were insistent. He pried the tense muscles apart, and found the slick hole at the center.

"Quite the little cockteaser, aren't you?" he said. "I'll bet you used to go around like this all the time in the world outside, driving men crazy, secure in the knowledge that the police had to protect you, the same police who would have loved to get on the line of men waiting to slide their cocks into your sperm-slick snatch. And all the while, I'll bet you wrote pieces about women's liberation, and how oppressive men were. And didn't you get your revenge, you hot little cunt? Didn't you make them sweat and squirm? Well, it may be time for some role reversal."

With that, he slipped the middle finger of his right hand into her asshole. She gasped and blushed. With his other hand, he yanked her skirt off. She was naked from the waist down with a man's hand in her ass.

"Move," he ordered.

"What?" she said.

In reply, he simply shoved forward and she was forced off balance. She began to walk. It was grotesque, humiliating, and highly stimulating to be marched around in front of everyone else in the square in that totally compromising position. With each step she took, his finger seemed to lodge more deeply in her asshole. Her cunt began to tingle and get moist. She was on the brink of a prelude to ultimate degradation. Several times she wanted to fling herself facedown and have him finger-fuck her and force her to take the next step in the stripping away of her self-consciousness. Added to that was the fact that he was so overwhelmingly attractive, and under other circumstances she would be kicking her legs to the heavens and rubbing her nipples and running her tongue over her lips and crying out until she was hoarse to have him shove more things into more of her holes.

"That would be called making love, perhaps because it takes place in a bed and the man and woman involved know one another's names. But here, what do I call it?" She was given over to one of those satori-type moments in which it is seen that what one does is beyond categories. For an instant, the entire structure of civilization fell away, including language. She was a life form, on the face of a huge rock in the middle of a mysterious and fathomless universe. Attached to her was another life form, and together they were doing an arcane dance the esoteric meaning of which might be unknown to all but a very few.

"Oh, it feels so-o-o-o good," Constance moaned, breaking out of her revery. The man pulled his finger out sharply and abruptly, and she quivered for half a minute, her ass cheeks contracted and trembling, her legs shivering, her tits shaking, her nipples wrinkled. At that moment she would have found it gratifying if a tank had rumbled into the arena, rumbled toward her, and wedged the barrel of its howitzer into her expanding cunt.

The man grabbed her shoulders and pushed her forward. He took her to the door which led out of the square. He marched her past the swimming pool where her passage was greeted by shocked glances or whistles and catcalls by the women lounging there. Halfway across the space, he spun her around and, crouching down, spread her legs apart. He formed his fingers into a V and shoved them quickly into her pussy. She went bowlegged to accommodate the entry. Once in up to the second knuckles, he curled his fingers and made a fist. She was fist-fucked standing up.

He then began to push his fist forward, forcing her to walk backward. She had to cover the hundred yards past the pool and tennis court, in full view of some fifty people, with the young man squatting in front of her, his fist covered by her cunt folds, as she staggered and stumbled backwards, ass thrusting and exposed.

He led her in that manner until they were some fifteen feet from the edge of the cliff and then he pulled his fist out as abruptly and harshly as he had pulled his finger out. Constance did a small dance around the sudden emptiness at her core and after a minute sank to her knees. She lay down, convinced he was going to fuck her, or subject her to some new indignity. Part of her was apprehensive, but part of her tingled in anticipation.

"Maybe your time is up, bitch," he said, closing in on her. His face was pure anger. "Maybe you've teased your last cock. Maybe it's time for you to meet your Unmaker."

For the first time since she had arrived at the Parlor, Constance was run through with a chill of serious terror. The man came to within a foot of her, then stopped. He looked down through slitted lids, and once again raised his hand and snapped his fingers. Four guards ran out of hiding and sprung to attention at his side.

"Rig up a drop," the man said.

Then, turning to Constance, he dropped to his knees beside her, and buried his face between her breasts.

"Oh Mommy, Mommy," he sobbed, "I'm sorry, Mommy." To her surprise, Constance felt hot tears on her tits. The man was crying loudly and wetly into her bosom, the tears soaking the thin material of her blouse. He tried to burrow more deeply into her, and tore the fabric away so he could clamp his mouth on one of her nipples. He sucked at it ferociously, and Constance hovered between pain and a species of hurting pleasure. There was nothing much to do, so she lay back and let him have his way.

She had lapsed into a dreamlike revery when the guards returned carrying a large wooden structure that looked like a frame for hanging. They struck one end of the vertical beam into a specially constructed hole at the very edge of the cliff. The horizontal beam now hung over the abyss, a rope dangling from its tip.

Constance looked at the device with horror.

"Oh no," she murmured. And then screamed, "Oh my God! No!" And tried to pull away and run. But the young man held her in an iron grip, his mouth glued to her nipple. She beat at him with her fists and finally he pulled away, smiling, cursing, and sobbing all at once. He didn't give the impression of a man who was responsible for his actions. When he stood up, Constance saw that he sported an enormous erection.

The guards pounced on her and held her down while one of them tied the rope around her ankles. Then she was carried to the edge of the cliff. She was too frightened to breathe. They counted to three, heaved, and threw her into the abyss. She closed her eyes and died a thousand deaths in that split second of falling before the rope caught and held her there, dangling, head down, four hundred feet above the rocks and surf.

She swung back and forth, dizzily, crazily. The cliff swam before her eyes, the shale, the tiny flowers, the grass, the bird's nest, all hyperrealistically etched into her brain like high contrast, precision photos. Below her, unimaginable horror and shattering death.

She looked up. The four guards were standing at the edge, looking down dispassionately. The young man was pointing down at her, laughing madly, slapping his knee and jumping up and down. She closed her eyes and resigned herself to her fate.

She swung a long time and came to a standstill. The day effected its closure around the hideous happening. Once again, it was a hot, quiet afternoon. Constance noticed that her nose itched.

She opened her eyes and looked up. The guards were gone, and the young man was sitting at the edge looking down at her. He had the same expression of artistic attention as he had shown when sketching her. It was almost a loving look.

"He's come full cycle," she thought. "A perfect psychotic, in complete identification with each of his aspects. And with no central self to inform the whole. The structure of enlightened beings and monsters."

The man was staring at her cunt, and Constance realized that she was completely exposed. Her tits hung upside down and almost came to her mouth. Her ass was an open gash for him to peer down into. She took a deep breath and calmed herself. It would be an interesting fall, and she imagined the impact itself wouldn't even be felt. She'd be unconscious before she felt pain. She'd be dead before she was unconscious.

"They told me I couldn't kill you," he said at last in a soft voice. "I wanted to know what made you so special."

"Who are *they*?" she wondered.

"But they didn't say I couldn't scare you." He paused and peered into her eyes. "Are you scared?"

"I was," she responded. "But I'm not any more. I suppose I should thank you. You cured me of my fear of death."

"Oh, I'm so glad," he said, unexpectedly, and for an instant she thought she detected a note of authenticity in his voice.

"You're very beautiful," he told her.

"It's the most bizarre circumstances for a compliment I've ever experienced," she thought, "but a girl can't be too choosy."

"I want to come in your mouth," he added.

"Why not?" she said to herself. "Just about everybody else has."

He dropped his pants and held his cock in his hands. He squinted over the bent top like a hunter looking down the barrel of a rifle. Constance looked up at him and a thrill of eerie companionship ran her. It had been a complex relationship, beginning with his exquisite portrait, going through his walking her around with his finger up her ass and then with his fist in her cunt, and flying with him through his changes from aesthete to sadist to little boy and back again. And now including his forcing her to look death in the face. She realized that she was quite turned on.

"I'd rather have you fuck me," she said.

"Later," he told her. "Tonight. In your room. Make it like a date. I like girls who put out. Dirty girls. Girls who like to have their cunts rubbed."

"All right," she said. "Later."

And then opened her mouth. And, hanging four hundred feet above her doom, suspended upside down over an abyss, she watched him masturbate slowly, and then more rapidly, until he was bringing himself off with reckless abandon, until the sperm shot out and curved in a long arc into space, splashing on her belly, on her tits, and finally on her lips, at which point she ran her tongue over her mouth and drank in the extraordinary gift from his loins.

6

"But what do they get out of it? I can understand the physical part, the simple use of a body for one's pleasure, and I can get some understanding of the psychological aspect, the fact of having someone tied down and helpless. It is enough to make a person feel like God. But all of that seems pretty superficial. I mean, for the money I imagine a man spends for a session in the Parlor, he could have a hundred different women blowing him on consecutive nights throughout an entire winter. Now that would be *real pleasure*. And the psychological part, well, it shouldn't take more than a moment's reflection and thought for a man to see through the game and discard it as unworthy of an adult."

Constance spoke slowly and languidly, pausing often to take puffs of a cigarette and blow clouds into the cloudless night. Robert lay on a chaise longue next to her. They were on her balcony, and it was two hours before she was scheduled to go on duty. He had dropped by an hour earlier to ask if he might visit for a while. She was glad of the distraction, for after a three-day rest the thought of going back into the Parlor was starting to create obsessive fear patterns in her mind. She'd fixed him a drink, and they had taken to the out-of-doors to enjoy the balmy air and the spectacle of the naked universe. Their talk had gone from the conventional to the specific to the personal in quick, easy stages until they arrived at the delicious level of true philosophical discourse, ruminations on the meanings of one's experience as an aspect of common human consciousness.

"You give a lot of undue credit, Constance," Robert replied. "The people who come here aren't capable, most of them, of reflection and thought. They are mere automata, with as much free will as marionettes on a string. They are the privileged wealthy, from all nations, all races, all cultures. They are the Noble Scum of the Earth, the ones through whom our destiny is shaped. When they enter the Parlor, they maintain as much consciousness as a mesmerized gambler at a craps table. As for pleasure, I'm sure that if one of them ever felt a true moment's pleasure, a real throbbing and melting and surrender, they would think it was some form of attack and run to see a doctor."

Constance smiled, although the corners of her mouth didn't go as far as they might, the movement being checked by her remembrance that she was due to be subjected within the hour to the very monsters they were discussing.

Robert watched her through lids that were almost closed. He was resting his eyes but also slipping into a posture of utter indifference so that Constance would be less on her guard.

"The next question you are going to ask, I'll bet," he said, "is, 'What's a nice guy like you doing in a place like this?'"

It was the first time since their initial meeting that he indicated by tone of voice or any other signal that he was still courting her in his peculiar fashion. She remembered his warning that sooner or later she would be hungry for a relationship, which combined the vibration she received from men in the Parlor with the tenderness and intimacy she had with Madge and the other women. And that when that time came, he would be there, waiting, ready to receive the full flowering of her new womanhood. She had come so far as to accept that that would indeed happen, but was taking her time about it, judging that keeping Robert at precisely the right distance was the best life insurance she could take out.

"No," she replied, "I know what you're doing here. And you know that I think that you are immeasurably lower than the swine who patronize the place. As you point out, they are largely too stupid to know what they're really doing. But you know exactly what you're doing, which is the first requisite of doing evil."

She stared at him as she spoke, and was surprised to notice that he flinched when she said the last word. She had said worse things to him with no noticeable effect, and she wondered why he had suddenly developed such a thin skin.

"Have I offended you?" she asked in mock innocence.

"Wounded," he replied.

"Really?" she drawled, smirking.

But when he replied, there was an infinitesimal tremor in his lower lip. "I've come to grow very fond of you, Constance, even in my monstrous fashion. And it shouldn't come as too big a surprise for you to learn that even monsters can be vulnerable."

"Yeah, I hear that Himmler used to weep when he listened to Chopin."

Again, at the reference to the Gestapo leader, Robert winced. Constance began to wonder whether he were a consummate actor or whether she were actually touching some chord in him, and whether that might be exploited. It was odd, however, that she now almost never thought of escape, but burned with a passion to know who was really running the place.

"I really ought to take you to my private parlor and work you over," he said in an incongruously light tone. "It might teach you some respect."

"Not to speak of a few new tricks," she quipped.

Their conversation turned on its edge, skirted the periphery of banter, and metamorphosed into silent mutual appreciation. She was constantly surprised at the ways in which she found herself liking the man.

"Speaking of which," she added, "who is that lunatic that grabbed me yesterday?"

Robert smiled grimly. "I heard about that," he said.

"Good God!" she exclaimed. "Do you realize he had me hanging by my heels forty storeys above the ground? Do you have any idea of what that feels like?"

"Did he show up for the date?"

"What?" She pretended not to understand.

"The women he ravishes usually fall for him," Robert went on. "And they agree to meet him later to make love. But he's never shown up as far as I know. I was wondering whether he made an exception in your case."

"And what makes you think . . . ?" she began indignantly, but couldn't go on with the pretense. She laughed. It was all the answer he needed.

"I frankly don't know who he is," Robert said after he had lit a cigarette and poured another daiquiri from the pitcher next to him. He was totally at ease, dressed only in tennis shorts and a linen T-shirt. Constance wore a thin cotton robe, but during the course of their talk it had worked itself open and now covered only part of one thigh, a portion of her pubic hair, and her right breast. She enjoyed the ambiguity of the garment, since nudity was no special event on the grounds nor clothes any mark of status. As he poured his drink, Robert took in the exposed curves of her body with his lidded eyes and his stare seemed to want to slither under those portions of cloth they couldn't get to in order to touch with jellylike avidity the membrane, hair, and flesh. Constance smiled to herself, proving her point that the direction of true eroticism was toward subtlety.

"All I know," Robert went on, "is that he has four armed guards as his *personal* entourage at all times, and that all the other guards have been ordered to give him absolute priority in any dispute arising from conflicting orders on any issue."

"Sounds like the boss's son," she said.

"The boss," Robert mused. "I wonder who that is?"

"How did you get this job?" she asked him.

"Answered an ad in the *Times*," he told her and then, seeing her beginning grin of disbelief, added, "It's true, honest to God. There was an ad for an 'Executive Assistant.' It offered high pay, pleasant surroundings, very interesting work, and indescribable fringe benefits. So I replied, and they tested me, screened me, put me through paces, fed information to me slowly, until they finally brought me here. Just before the departure I had been told that once I arrived at the job site itself I would know too much to ever be allowed to quit the organization and did I want to leave then? As I told you, the promise of money, leisure, dictatorial power over others, and a supply of women whom I might use as slaves sounded like the fulfillment of my most cherished childhood dream."

"And what keeps you from escaping?" she asked. "I don't mean just you, but people in your position? I'm sure that one of the stewards or attendants or even the guards has tried to get away."

"Escape is impossible," he said flatly. "Of course, the idea of escape is essential. There is always that percentage of the population that needs its myth of reassurance. And so the 'revolution' among the women is tolerated and even smiled upon. The notion of having to get into orgies in order to whisper secrets to one another behind the screen of moans and cries is a priceless gem, actually. A perfect wedding of sex and politics."

Constance's mouth dropped open. "You know about that?" she asked, aghast.

"Everything is known that can be known," he said. "And that which can't be known either doesn't exist or is beyond our ability to know it. Yes? Why struggle in a masque of naivety?"

"And what do you know about me?"

"That you will be predictable," he said. "You will explore all the games available here, the erotic, the political, the personal, the theatrical. You will take notes in your head and try to puzzle out who the boss really is. And you will wait your opening for escape. No opening will ever take place. You will have your affair with me, during which you will probably try to take my life one time. And finally, after an indeterminate period of time, you will be too

70

scarred and too hard and too tired and too much overdue, and then you will be scheduled for the Snuff."

He drained the contents of his glass, took a long puff on his cigarette, paused for the desired effect, which was to fix her attention one hundred percent, and then added, "Or . . ."

She leapt right to the bait. "Or?" she repeated.

Robert laughed. "Caught you, didn't I?" He gave her a few seconds to wonder whether she'd been cruelly tricked and then said, "Or we might consider taking you on to the staff."

She sucked her breath in. Robert smiled, his lips thin.

"Interesting, isn't it?" he asked.

"You son of a bitch," she spat at him. "You *would* tempt me with something like that."

"Of course," he replied.

"To exchange an innocent slavery for an evil slavery. To become one of the masters, slaves who are foolish enough to think they are free. And for what? To live another twenty . . . thirty . . . forty years?"

"That's all there is, isn't there?"

"I must admit I haven't been asked the question in such immediate and serious circumstances before."

"How long do you think you'd require for an answer?"

"It would probably depend on the measure of my extremity at the time the offer was made, quite frankly."

"Bien entendu," he replied.

There was a silence such as surrounds the growth and maturation of mushrooms and cucumbers, the quiet which attends the consciousness continually forming at the very edge of life's appearance into the material cosmos.

They remained for several minutes, floating in the shards of space, lurching like great cakes of ice broken loose from the great floes that cover the poles. The awareness of their mood held the sort of mammoth sluggishness felt by tusked and shaggy elephants in the white din of the long Arctic night. They sank far beneath the surface identity of human and human, male and female, and tapped into the eternal fact of raw unstructured life, sentient, awake, infinite.

Outside that awareness, in the narrative of their behavior, a small breeze had sprung up to dust their skins like a delicately applied powder puff. Slowly, Constance stretched and pulled herself out of the free-floating state into which she had drifted.

"I think I just had an out-of-the-body experience," she said.

"How about an in-the-body experience?" he asked.

She looked at him. Boyish, perfect features, a trim, tanned body. She enjoyed his mind and had no doubt but that he would be an exquisite lover. But to accept him would be to go over the final edge, to have that last ledge of inner autonomy crumble and for her to go flying into the arms of a new reality. It was something like giving up the citizenship of one's native country to become a denizen of a foreign land, yet a land which has come to seem to the wanderer to offer a haven for dreams which one had, since childhood, despaired of ever having come true, but dreams which flew in the face of all one's conscious, social training. If she gave herself to Robert, she would have to say good-bye to Chet, and to a Constance that had crystallized around a different matrix of constancy.

"I'm on duty soon," she said.

Robert rolled to his feet and padded into the bedroom. He picked up the house phone, said a few words into it, and walked back to her.

"I found you a substitute," he said.

"That's not fair," she replied. "I can't let you do that to one of the other girls."

"We have a special stand-by team," he told her. "We call it the cow pen."

Her breasts rose and fell as she breathed a sigh of release. Some deep tension inside her gave way and she succumbed to that part of her which she had always known existed and yet had always denied. And now that she accepted it, owned it as herself, she was astonished to realize that it had always formed the central focus for her understanding of life. And precisely because she had blocked herself from acknowledging it, she had spent most of her years living in a kind of sleep. What had taken place struck no analogy so strongly as that of the Jew in the concentration camp taking on the role of minor functionary in order to save his life. Constance was going to go further; she was going to fall in love with the Nazi colonel.

For love it would have to be. Robert was too sophisticated a task master, too subtle an observer for him to allow her to sham the emotion.

"Well, how do we proceed?" she asked looking up at him.

"We go to my room," he told her.

"It's just like the my-place-or-yours cliché that used to run around the singles' bars," she said. "But I've never been to your room. It will be a romance."

"Of sorts," he told her, smiling strangely, his lips twisted into the shape one might expect of a mouth that had just tasted its first shreds of human flesh.

She put a cloak on over her robe and followed Robert down a succession of hallways until they reached a check point where a guard stood, rifle over his shoulder, to let them pass. They went into a section Constance had never seen before, and Robert explained that this was where the entire staff was housed. They got into an elevator and got off at the fifth floor. Robert had a complete suite to himself. He showed Constance in to a huge living room with a magnificent view of the sea. To one side there was a kitchen, and a bath led off a small hallway at the opposite corner.

"Where's the bedroom?" she asked after he had taken her cloak, fixed her a drink, and showed her the view.

"In a hurry?" he teased, running his fingers through her hair.

She leaned her head back against his hand and began to purr. His hand slid down, between her shoulder blades, down her spine, over her ass, and probed the crack between her buttocks gently. She tensed, relaxed, and then tensed again. It had been such a long time since she felt a man begin to make love to her. After the rigors of the Parlor and the pleasantries of the scenes with the women, it was an overwhelming luxury to sink into the old-fashioned associations connected with simple sex. He slid behind her, his hand now slipping around her front and going up to cup and fondle her breasts, his other hand stroking her thighs and cupping the hairy protrusion of bone and moist mucous membrane which constituted the overall gestalt of cunt.

She leaned back and rested against the front of his body, his already rising cock nestling into the soft ridge between her ass cheeks. She let her lips part and began to breathe through her mouth, one of the first signs of erotic excitation. Perhaps the central reason why those who have taken and who teach what is popularly considered a "spiritual" path have taken such a hard line on sex, is that while fucking, people fly into shallow and chaotic breathing, a state of affairs totally contrary to the teaching that one should breathe through one's nose, calmly, and into the belly, with long regular rhythmic breaths.

She spun around and gazed fiercely into his eyes.

"If I let go, if I give myself to you, you will have my soul. You know that, don't you?"

"The price you pay for saving your life. I believe it's a fairly classic bargain."

"Do I have to sign the contract in blood?" she quipped.

"Yes," he replied simply.

She took his answer as a return jibe and dismissed it. She put her arms behind his head, her elbows resting on his shoulders. She pressed the front of her body against his. Her face was only a few inches away from his.

"Take me," she said.

He looked at her for a few seconds the way a man might examine the gun he was about to use to blow his brains out, and then closed his eyes and covered her mouth with his. The instant their lips met, they ignited, fused, and burned with an irresistible flame. Heat began to radiate from them and fill the room. The mirrors strained to be looked into and the rug blushed. His hands roamed up and down the back of her freely.

"Oh, I adore the way you touch me freely," she moaned.

His kiss went on a long time, long after she had gone slack and simply let him have his feel of her mouth. She had a fleeting recollection of Henry who had wanted this from her and had her tied in order to use her lips at will. It occurred to her that Robert also had her tied, if not with ropes then with the power of life and death he held over her.

"Maybe the only way a man can really feel comfortable with a woman is if he feels he has her under his complete domination," she thought and began remembering all the men she had been with to check out the startling hypothesis. There were times when a man wanted a woman to be all activity, to moan and writhe and go mad with the sensations she was feeling, to let it all hang out. And times when he wanted them both to be lost in the same flow of movement. To lose distinction between self and other in the joyous melting of the give-and-take. But there were also those times when a man definitely wanted the woman just to lie there and be a source stimulus for his desire and otherwise to keep out of the way, not to move, speak, or even look.

"I can understand that," she said. "There are times when I want the same from men." It suddenly occurred to her that there was no difference between men and women in relation to what they wanted. The only argument was that they went to war over the available resources. In the same way that people are the same all the world over, everyone wanting happiness and well-being, all men and women want gratification in bed. And to get it, they are ready to go to terrific extremes, with men resorting to physical force and women calling on all the wiles of their emotional storehouses.

"Now, Constance," Robert whispered. "Now that you are totally open, your body relaxed, your senses reeling, your mind romping in the wilds of its own game preserve, now you must look at me and see that I see you, and accept that seeing, acknowledge it, feel it penetrate to your center. And you must suddenly and fiercely forge your entire identity on that instant in which our truths touch, and pledge that no other voice within you shall ever take precedence before the one now speaking . . . the combination of our consciousnesses as embodied in the sound of my voice. And you must say, 'Yes,' and gasp and utter a little cry of ultimate discovery and fling your mouth onto mine and lose yourself in my arms and rub against me and want to turn your cunt inside out all over my tongue and cock and fingers. Then you must whisper endearments, and say things like, 'My darling,' or 'Precious one,' and cling to me as though I were a mighty oak in a hurricane, your only protection against being swept away by the storm. And yet know that within me there are realms of terror and chaos which make actual storms appear the stuff of fairy tales."

"Robert, I love you," she said.

74

He picked her up in his arms and strode with her across the length of the room to the bookcase at the far end. Once there, he pressed a tiny lever on the wall with his foot and the bookcase slid to one side, revealing a door that opened into a dark room.

"Now we're ready for the bedroom," he said.

As they moved into the space, Constance thought to herself, "I did it. I fooled him. But in doing it, I had to fool myself. I believed what I was saying, even if only for those few seconds. And now I must travel the thin edge of this new ambiguity."

Robert put her down and she stood there for a few seconds, blinking. There were peculiar sounds in the space, muted whimperings. Abruptly, she was terrified. And at the instant of recognizing the feeling, the light went on.

"Oh my God," Constance gasped.

It was a large, cavernous chamber. The walls were made of stone, cut right into the cliff against which the building was built. The space was like a museum of medieval horrors. All the implements of torture were there: the rack, the pincers, the thumbscrews, the open fireplace with a roasting spit over it, whips, a cauldron for boiling oil, and numberless other fiendish results of heated imaginations. Along one wall hung three oversized bird cages. In each one crouched a naked woman. The women were dirty, scratched, and the bottoms of their cages hadn't been cleaned for some time, so that they sat in their own excrement and urine. Robert went over and banged on the cages with a stick, rousing them from their stupors.

"Feeding time!" he sang out. He turned to Constance. "You'll excuse me a second, won't you? I've been very neglectful of my pets. Have a seat. Get comfortable. There, there's a chair you can use."

Constance backed away until she had come to the leather chair and then sank into it with all the relief of a child finding its mother after being lost for half an hour. She watched with eyes that were glued open as Robert took a hose and washed out the cages, playing the water over the women who made pitiful efforts to scrub themselves while the water washed over them. Then, when he had finished, he filled three bowls with what looked like a kind of gruel and slipped them into slots at the bottoms of the cages. The women, to her dismay, buried their faces in the slop and sucked it up voraciously. She realized they must have been famished. When they finished, they slid the bowls back outside.

"Can't you at least give them spoons?" Constance asked.

"I like to see them eat like dogs," he told her. "When I take them out and put them in harness it retains the consistency of realism."

She looked at him with an appeal in her eyes.

"They are here," he said, forestalling the words that went with her look, "because they undertook to accept my offer. I took each of them on as a mistress at one time or another, and they all disappointed me. I told them the rules, the stakes, and the penalties, and they agreed to gamble. For my part, I have kept my promise. They are all exempt from the Snuff."

"It makes one wonder whether that isn't preferable," she said, her aplomb beginning to return.

"Good," he said, "I'm beginning to see some color in your cheeks again. And yes, it does make one wonder. But there it is, my dear. You can go back to the ranks, do your stint several times each week, live as luxuriously as you want, and wait that day which, after all, must come to everyone. Or you can try to make it to a staff level by pleasing me, in which case, after a while, you will get your own room and duties. But if you fail me, then I will put you in one of those cages, and treat you the way people treat their pet birds. Although I must tell you that I am usually more conscientious about keeping the cages clean and the ladies fed."

"One thing I must say about you, Robert. You certainly know how to present a lady with a challenge."

"Otherwise, what's the fun of living? Yes?" He said the last word less as a question than as an invitation for her to join him in the complicity of his deeds and viewpoint.

"Compassion may indeed be the opiate of the congenitally weak," she thought. "Maybe those who are ruthless enough to take what they want find exhilaration from total disregard of what pain they cause others. Maybe cruelty is a valid way of getting high."

Yet, even as she formulated the thoughts, she heard another voice, that of an old teacher, telling her that a person was free to choose whatever way of life he or she wanted. Existentialism was accurate thus far. But that there was also a real truth of what a human being was, and that to use one's free choice to become other than that simply marked the person as a cretin, not worthy of discussion or consideration by any mature man or woman.

And even as that voice trailed off, yet a third arose to note that the three women were going to stay in their cages no matter what she did. It was foolish to think of liberating them. They had chosen their own doom. So her choice had to be based on no other consideration than whether she could be successful in meeting Robert's criteria.

"I'll try," she said. "What do you want me to do?"

"Ah!" he replied. "Your first task in pleasing me is finding out what pleases me. I am going to put you in the role of the male who is attracted to a woman. How rare is the woman who will tell him how and where she likes to be stroked, or who will make his task of exploration easier, or who will instruct him in the intricacies of her timing? No, the man must lavish the totality of his entire range of performance upon her, so that she, like a bored countess at a fete, may nibble at her discretion . . . a bite of cheese, a spoon of caviar, a sip of champagne, and a peeled pear, perhaps. And when it is over, give him no indication other than a rolling of the eyes to indicate that his spilling his seed for her did or did not satisfy her for the nonce."

As he finished speaking, he lay down on a wide mattress covered with a satin sheet, his ankles crossed, his hands behind his head.

"Do me!" he said, smiling, and added, "I'm predisposed to give you a good grade because I truly am fond of you. But if you prove useless, then I'll have no choice but to hang you up."

"What mark do I have to make?"

"Anything below a B+ fails," he said.

"Can it really be," she wondered, "that I am standing in a cave with a strange man, with three naked women locked in cages hanging from the ceiling, prepared to find some way to titillate his totally jaded faculties in order to win myself a position as a slave overseer, or to find myself caged for life in this sunless room?" She took a deep breath and looked around. "Yes, indeed, it not only can be, but is," she concluded.

As for Robert, she knew that there was only one approach even worth trying, and that was one of absolute insouciance. She had to attain the state of one hypnotized and convinced that the circumstances were other than they were. Memories of method acting classes came to mind.

The worst thing to do would be to try to rouse him by some form of erotic melodrama. She had fleeting images of tying him, flogging him, fucking him with a dildo, sucking his cock for three hours, pouring an excess of sensation on him. Instead, she simply shrugged and slipped out of her negligee. She stood before him, naked and easy. She used no wiles, no artifacts, no little bits of theatre. Rather, she gathered within herself the totality of her courage, her awareness, her vulnerability, and then dressed herself in those realities. She stood before him, in short, in the blazing thusness of her womanhood, and hurled the full impact of that down upon him.

She watched his cock get hard inside his trunks. She watched desire-smoke curl in his eyes. She watched the facade of disinterest crack and crumble.

Then, when she had shown him the essence, the whole; when she forced him to accept the fact that she saw him with the same intensity with which he saw her, that she was his equal . . . *only* THEN did she let him have the specific-part pleasures.

Then she slipped her hands under her breasts and offered the nipples to him. She slid her fingers down between her thighs and opened her cunt lips for him to look at. She turned around so he could admire her ass and imagine what his cock would look and feel like slipping in and out of her asshole. She ran her tongue over her lips and tripped him out with promises of oral paradise.

It was, up to that point, a performance which had the advantage of distance. She was not committed in the sense that any sign of his losing interest could spur her into transforming what she was doing into foreplay. But now she had to take the final step. She walked forward, she sat down on the bed, she lay down on her back next to him, she took a deep breath, relaxed into the soft mattress, and then closed her eyes.

She waited what seemed an eternity before she felt his breath on her throat, and heard his voice, low and vibrant, say, "I been waiting for a woman like you for a long time."

She opened her eyes. Robert licked her throat, kissed her ear, and brought his face over hers. She looked directly into his gaze.

"Perfect," he whispered. "Cool, smart, brave, beautiful. And you know how to play the Game." He paused, as though he were swallowing something, and then said, "And now I am going to fuck you, and take you home."

She closed her eyes again and gave herself up to what followed. She felt his brief struggle to remove his shorts. Then he was all over her. His mouth on and in hers, his hands inside her cunt. She sighed and opened her legs. He felt her with the delicate obscenity of a true lover. He not only stroked the insides of her cunt, relishing each fold, each bump, each new evidence of secretion; he not only whipped his fingers around until the cavern was filled with froth; he not only rolled the flesh between his fingers like a tailor estimating the quality of a piece of cloth; but he did it all in a way that made her feel that he felt that she felt precisely what he wanted her to feel, or rather, knew that she had to be feeling given the manner of his manipulations. He had her, and he knew it, and wanted her to give herself not only to the sensations, or even to him, but to the fact of his mastery in the moment.

She capitulated. And then they were making love. They clung to one another and embraced fiercely and rivaled an entire nation with the hunger expressed in their kisses. Now when his hand slipped over her ass and his finger slid into the hole, there was no gap between the instant of penetration and the instant of response. His entry and her reception were simultaneous as psychic events. She raked his back with her nails and cried to have his cock inside her.

He rolled her face down and trembled over her for a few moments. Her loveliness was breathtaking. Long smooth back flaring into arched, taut buttocks, and between: the dark, the moist, the invitation to hair and heat and wet; and below all that, two shapely legs, now kicking ever so slightly in a scissors motion of muted excitement. He lowered his body onto hers, swimming in the sweet surrender of the contact. She rose up almost imperceptibly to meet him, her ass twitching.

He put his hands over her eyes.

78

"Where are you?" he asked.

"I don't know," she told him. "Anywhere."

"Who are you?" he asked.

"I don't know," she replied. "Anyone."

"And what do you want?"

"I don't know," she said. "Anything."

"The Parlor?" he whispered. "Do you enjoy the Parlor?"

"Yes," she sobbed. "Anything. Just so long as I am being touched, being entered. I don't care. I just want my cunt stuffed, my ass touched, my mouth stimulated. And I want my heart to come alive."

"Then love me."

"No, please," she begged.

"Love me," he repeated.

Now his cock was hard and he slipped it between her thighs. The top of it rubbed against the outside of her cunt. She arched her buttocks and pressed more tightly against him. She began to rotate her hips and went after him with a touch of desperation. He pulled back slightly. She moaned and thrust her ass back to maintain the contact. Abruptly, he went to his knees. She whimpered and went to her knees, kneeling in front of him, rump offered. He grabbed her ass cheeks, the thumbs near the hole, the other fingers on the outside, and pulled them apart. She cried out and put her face on the bed, completing her posture of submission. He held the left cheek open with his left hand and with his right hand grabbed his cock and rubbed it up and down the crack, slipping into the asshole and cunt with brief thrusts each time he passed.

"Ooohhhh," she moaned. She was overcome not only by the sensations of the moment, the delicious tantalizing teasing of the proffered cock, but also by the nostalgia of remembering what it had once been like. Her situation had been so extraordinary that the most common of all erotic experiences emerged as exotic. She hadn't realized how hungry she had become for the familiar.

Without planning or foreseeing it, tears sprang to her eyes. Hot, wet, compelling, they overflowed and ran in streams down her cheeks. Her face wrinkled and shrunk as she sobbed out her grief, while below and behind she waggled her ass and silently begged to be split apart with Robert's hard cock.

But he rolled her over once more and now she was on her back facing him. She tried to cover her face with her hands but he held her wrists. He did not let go until she knew she would have to keep her arms at her sides. She cried even more harshly, sobbing openly. He watched her fall apart and he smiled. And as the tears spilled, all the feelings connected to them came to the surface, all the emotions she had been suppressing in order to remain hard enough to survive. Now she was stripped bare by the loneliness, the fear, the confusion, the screeching despair of her situation. She wanted to be free, to run back into the world, into her old life. She wanted to walk down a street, to buy a frankfurter at a corner stand, to hear the voices of her friends, to see Chet again.

She opened completely, weeping, thrashing about, giving herself up to her sadness. Robert gazed on her, his eyes on fire. This was what he wanted; this is what all the men who paid so much for slaves really wanted. Not the cries of physical pain, not the bondage of physical constraints, not the penetration of fist-fucking, but to have, to savor, the actual authentic openness of a woman. To see her flailing about unself-consciously, so intent on her grief that she forgets she is naked, forgets that her tits are flopping madly, that her cunt is exuding thick aromas of dripjuice, that the ass is clenching and unclenching on the wrinkled sheets.

When she reached the pinnacle of her wail, he leaned forward, covered her mouth with his, and slid his cock slowly and deliciously into her open, wet, hot hole.

"Ohhhh noooo!" she yelled into the cavern of his mouth, suddenly aware that he had swooped in and taken her at her absolutely most vulnerable moment.

In response, he drew back and slammed his cock home.

She was caught halfway between her own expression and her reaction to his expression. Which was exactly where he wanted her. He had her in perfect vulnerability.

"Give it to me," he whispered. "Give me that juicy pussy, baby. And give me the whole woman that goes with it. Now! Go crazy on my cock!"

She hesitated for one microsecond, and then wrapped herself around him. Her arms locked around his back, her legs locked around his thighs. She closed her eyes. And then went wild. She went absolutely berserk, scratching, clawing, thrusting, bucking, sailing, pounding, thrusting, engulfing, swallowing, shouting. She became the quintessence of every last pornographic ideal, the voracious woman, shameless in her shamelessness for indiscriminate degradation in her need to be filled.

Robert smiled, relaxed, and enjoyed the ride. She sucked at him with her cunt for almost half an hour before the sperm was drawn violently from his body. He projected every imaginable smutty image on her as she labored to steal his ejaculation. And she just went on and on, a fucking machine, a lust pot, a crazed slut.

When he came, she shuddered for five minutes in sympathetic orgasm, crying out in the simple wonder of her realization of what she had just done, what she had become in the process. And when she finished shuddering,

Robert pulled out. Then he rolled over and lay on his back. After a few moments, he pulled out a cigarette and lit it.

"That was nice," he said, blowing out smoke.

"I'd forgotten what it could be like, just to let go."

"You're a pretty hot woman," he told her, idly reaching over to stroke her cunt, slipping one finger into the lips and twirling the slimy juices around. She twitched as he teased her.

"Just a woman," she amended. And then added, "Just a person. I don't want so much different from anyone else. Some affection, some special handling every once in a while."

She looked around the room, taking in the implements of torture, and her eyes fell on the three cages. The women were watching her intently, their eyes boring through the dim light.

"Oh my God," Constance said. "I'd forgotten all about them."

"You shouldn't," Robert replied. "They add a definite piquancy to the happenings."

She shuddered.

He laughed.

"You'll have to get used to such things if you are going to join the staff."

"You mean I have the job?" she said, her voice a thick mixture of sarcasm and false enthusiasm.

"If you want it," he replied seriously. "It's a rather big step, isn't it?"

"To become one of the slavers . . ." she mused. "And yet, the alternative is grim." She stretched. "It sure is good not to have to think about going to the Parlor again."

"Oh you'll go again," he said. "But this time as an overseer."

Robert reached out to stub his cigarette out in the ashtray next to the bed and then reached behind the night table to push a button. The doors of the three cages flew open and the women let themselves out with the ease of acrobats. Suddenly, they no longer seemed like emaciated, weak, starving, abused women. They walked toward the bed, smiling.

"Joan, June, and Emma," Robert said. "Also staff members."

"What . . . ?" Constance exclaimed.

"I merely set up the drama of the cages to test your responses, that's all. I really would have had no use for you if you had stormed out of here at the sight of them."

"You mean you had to test my hardheartedness?" Constance said with a trace of bitterness.

"No, your judgment," he replied. "I expected you to feel for them, but I also hoped that you would understand that there was nothing you could do and change your attitude at once."

81

"Hi," the three women said and climbed onto the bed.

"How nice," Robert sighed, and then lay back. "Go to it, ladies. Do your licking, and stroking, and fingering. Fill the room with the aroma of cunt juice and then cover me with your sweet, sweet flesh."

"I'm on my way up in the slave world," Constance thought. "I've made it to the harem of a minor functionary." And then surrendered to the mounting tremors of excitement and lust.

7

It was her first time in the Parlor as an employee and, she realized, the first time without a blindfold. Her first evening involved no specific task; she was to act as a "floater," moving about the room and being of assistance to any of the attendants who needed her. After her evening with Robert, when she and the three women had spent hours rolling about in the opulence of an excess of woman-flesh and he had taken his turns fucking each of them, climaxing the evening by having them kneel at the edge of the bed, four asses up and four cunts open and dripping, and walking behind them, slipping his cock into one cunt and then another, switching from pussy to asshole, and then ordering them to converge on his cock with their mouths, lying back as they swarmed over him with tongues and lips . . . after waking up the following morning, she was taken by one of the women to a new wing of the building, given an orientation talk, assigned a new room, and heartily welcomed aboard. She had had the day free to sleep and wash and get used to her new quarters, and then had gone on duty.

She was now dressed in a pair of green shorts, cut very tight, and a green T-shirt. She learned that this was the standard uniform for lower-level workers in the Parlor. She walked around in a trance, trying to assimilate the sights which went with the sounds she had grown so used to. It was difficult. For everywhere she looked, she saw women being subjected to the rigors that had been her fate until just the day before. And she still burned with the shame of betrayal, the inner voice, which whispered that she had sold out and was now to be numbered among the lowest form of life on earth. And yet, what else could she do? She would not be assisting a single person by remaining a slave. While in her new capacity, she might at least have the possibility of helping someone in some way as yet undefined.

"Constance, over here please," she heard a voice say.

She went where she was called. Roger, one of the attendants, was tying a woman down to one of the tables. It was a tall girl whose body hair had been entirely removed. Not only her arms and legs and underarms, but her eyebrows and the hair on her head and cunt. Then she had been rubbed with a body oil, and covered with a white creme so that she looked like an alabaster statue. The attendant was tying her with white silk cords onto a slab of blood-red leather. The contrast was staggeringly powerful.

"What is it, Roger?" Constance asked.

"She's brand new," Roger said. He was a short black man in his early fifties. He'd been working for the Slavers for almost thirty years and was universally liked for his friendliness and kindness. "And she's probably a little bit more terrified than is good for her or for business. Maybe you can calm her a bit."

The girl had been given a local muscle paralyser so that her jaw was tight and she couldn't talk. Her eyes were wide with fear as she gazed all around her.

"Why no blindfold?" Constance asked.

"Client wants to see the terror in her eyes," Roger replied matter-of-factly.

Constance went over and stood next to the table. The girl was breathtakingly beautiful. Nearly six feet tall, thin, with the muscles of a ballet dancer. Her breasts were high and full, although as she now lay they fell to either side of her torso. The nipples were rouged to stand out against the marble skin. The only other spots of color were her eyes, which were jet-black, and the insides of her cunt, a coral pink turning out against the whitened outer lips. She trembled finely from head to toe like a colt in a light rain. She was a superb creature, and probably not too many days over seventeen years old.

"A week ago she was probably dating the captain of the football team in her home town," Constance thought. And then speculated that no one the girl had come into contact with up to that moment had had the foggiest notion of what to do with her. Probably all the boys she saw had vague and brooding fantasies of fucking her or having her suck their cocks, but couldn't refine the notion any further. And now, all at once, she was in the hands of some of the most sophisticated erotic engineers in the world, being subjected to a barrage of stimulation which the poor girl wouldn't have had the imagination to even conceive of.

Constance reached over and took the girl's hand in her own. The girl turned her head and looked up at her. Her eyes were indeed filled with fear. She tried to work her jaw, to say a few words. But she couldn't, and in a few seconds the tears flowed down her cheeks.

"Damn," Roger muttered, "that's going to spoil the makeup."

He handed a tissue to Constance who then sponged the tears up from the girl's cheek. The girl shot her a look of supplication, wanting Constance to help her in some way. Constance's reaction appalled her. She felt her belly tremble, and something let go in her crotch and the next thing she knew her cunt was getting wet. She suddenly realized that she was in a position of real power. Her power, of course, was limited, but she was able to make some changes in the reality which would effect the tied girl radically.

All at once the vista of power opened before her. She saw that if she were on top, really on top, with money and guns at her command, then she would be able to have slaves of her own. She would be able to command the loyalty of other human beings, to have them work for her, fuck for her, to kill them if she wished. It occurred to her that all her benevolent impulses had been based on the awareness of herself as a powerless person, someone fairly near the bottom of the heap. She had had no choice but to be nice. But if she were wealthy, possessed of money and connections, then she could be as she wished: cruel, disdainful, haughty, capricious, hard.

She checked the impulse she had to stroke the cheek of the girl who was looking up at her. "She would look at anyone in my position with those puppy-dog eyes," Constance thought. "There is no such thing as individuated personality. There is only the role within which the energy takes shape. She is helpless and I have power, and that is the only matrix of any meaning."

Constance reached over and tweaked one of the girl's nipples. The girl gasped and looked up at Constance with confusion. Constance smiled, and the smile said, "You thought you would find comfort in me, but you find only another master."

Out loud, she said, "When the man is finished with you, I will take you to my room and have you for myself. Do you understand? If you do, blink twice. And then perhaps I will help make you comfortable during your ordeal. Otherwise, you will get nothing but further torment from me."

The girl stared up and then blinked twice.

"That's good," Constance said, and ran her hand down the lithe frame and over the hairless cunt. She inserted one finger into the pink slit and moved it around until she had gathered a thin slick of pungent slime. Then she pulled

85

the finger up and brought it to the girl's mouth, and slipped it between her lips. The girl tried to pull away.

"Lick it," Constance said. "Lick your own cunt juice off my finger."

She felt the girl's tongue hesitantly come up and lick her finger, like a cat lapping at a finger dipped in milk. The girl's eyes showed mortification, and Constance smiled again and pushed her finger down on the girl's tongue.

"Do you like to eat your own pussy?" she said.

"Mmm, mm!" Roger said. "You sure do learn fast. Wasn't too long ago you was one of the slaves and now you are starting to talk just like one of the masters."

"I'm still a slave," Constance said. "The only difference is that I have a slightly better position inside the slave quarters, that's all."

"We used to call them 'house niggers,'" Roger said.

"Hey, I want her absolutely virginal," a voice rang out.

Constance turned and saw a short pudgy man approach. He was in his forties, dressed in a suit pants and white shirt with no tie. He wore slippers. He had obviously just come from his room. He walked brusquely up to the table and looked down at the quivering girl.

"Fantastic!" he muttered. "Delicious. What a juicy piece of pussy. Look at those tits! Man! What a feast!"

He looked reproachfully at Constance. "What were you doing to her?"

"Giving her a little taste of her own pussy juice," Constance said.

For an instant the man began to flash resentment that his slave had been tampered with, but then he began to chuckle. "Yeah," he said, "not a bad idea. Why don't you stick around? You can help me work her over. That would be fun. Watching her eat pussy."

The man pulled off his shirt and his pants and kicked off his slippers. He had a cock all out of proportion to the rest of his body, hanging like a small club under his bulging belly. The girl, who had never seen a cock before, began to tremble violently. The man laughed once, harshly, and then literally flung himself onto the table. He couldn't seem to get enough. Like someone who had been starving and suddenly pushed into a restaurant, the man tried to stuff everything into his mouth at once. He mauled her tits and pummeled her cunt; he crushed her mouth with his and slid his hands under her to cup her ass. He slid down and buried his face between her thighs to lap at her cunt and then scooted up and knelt at her head and forced his now erect cock into her frozen mouth.

Her eyes bulged and her lips curved obscenely over the thick phallus. It was impossible to tell what she was thinking or feeling. She provided a grotesque picture, her tawny, chalk-white form straining against her bonds, in stunning contrast to the red leather underneath, while the strange man fucked her mouth with harsh, long strokes.

86

"Finger-fuck her," the man gasped. "Get her hot!"

The idea that the poor girl could get "hot" under such circumstances seemed, to Constance, to betray the typical male misinterpretation of what a woman's sexuality was about. But hers was not to reason why, just to do so as not to die. She applied herself to the task. She pulled the girl's cunt lips apart, and peered into the center.

"She really does have a pretty pussy," Constance thought. "Young, fresh, virginal." And as she looked, she felt her own cunt starting to secrete with serious gushings. She slipped one finger into the girl's snatch and moved it slowly around. At first the response she received she ascribed to the fact that the girl was trying to pull away. But after a while, she realized that the girl was responding to the excitement she was feeling. Constance rubbed the elastic walls and probed the tender knob of the cervix. She prodded deep into the intimate recesses of the girl's most private part and reveled in the sense of desecration she was involved in. She drew her finger back and stroked the silky clitoris.

A moan escaped the girl, muffled as it was by the cock filling her mouth.

"Yeah, that's it," the man said. "Now she's starting to turn on a little bit," And then, dropping his voice to a kind of conspiratorial conversational tone, he went on to Constance, "It's no fun just fucking the body, you know. The thing you want to do is to wake them up. And make them really feel what they're doing. You know? Make an *impression* on them. Now, a chick like this, on the outside, would never give me a second glance. She'd be running around with some clod of a football player who'd be rubbing her pussy through her jeans in the front seat of a car. And I'd look at her and think, 'I'd love to ram my big cock down your throat,' but know I'd never get the chance. Then I found out about this place, and now I have the chance."

Constance continued her finger-fucking and the girl began to move her pelvis, to thrust back against Constance's thrusts. Constance realized that within a few hours she could have the girl all to herself. The girl was now moaning steadily and from the way the man was acting it seemed to Constance that the girl must be licking his cock with a frantic action of her tongue.

"That's it, that's it," the man crooned and then slipped his hands under the girl's head. For a long time he hunched over her, fucking her mouth, while Constance brought her to climax after climax with her fingers. It occurred to her that this was the first time the girl had ever had someone else's hand inside her.

"Now, now, now!" the man shouted and exploded inside the girl's mouth. He pulled back slightly so he could watch the sperm pulsing from the head of his cock and cascading down the girl's throat, over her tongue, onto her lips, until she was thick and sticky with hot jism. Then he pushed the spunk with his fingers, getting every bit in her mouth and forcing her mouth closed and holding it until he saw that she had swallowed every last drop.

He looked down a long time. The girl's eyes were opened wide, but instead of terror, what showed there was a kind of voluptuous disgust. She had just had something done to her that a few days earlier would have been the cause for permanent and massive trauma, and was now discovering that she had enjoyed it. The man saw all the changes in her eyes and gloated. His viewpoint had been vindicated. Although he was incapable of articulating it with any precision, he felt that a cunt was a blind and indiscriminate hole and responded to any stimulation it received, and that women's insistence on the relationship with the person attached to the object of stimulation was sheer sentimental prejudice.

"I'm going to take a rest," he said, hopping off the table, "and then I want her rolled over. I want to work on her pretty little ass next."

"You can take a break," Roger said to Constance as he stepped forward to undo the girl's bonds and clean her up for the next round. "There's a coffee shop through that door there."

"I need some air," Constance said. "I'm going to take a short walk."

She threaded her way through the crowd heading for the exit door, but before she reached it she felt a hand on her arm. She turned to face her accoster and found a tall, thin man in his early fifties grinning at her.

"You don't recognize me, do you?" he asked.

"No," she said.

"Last time we met, you had a blindfold on. I shoved the big end of a baseball bat up your ass." He waited a second. "Do you remember now?" he asked, like a teenage boy ready to be hurt.

"I can't say that you are familiar," she told him, "but I'd recognize your baseball bat anywhere."

The man laughed. "No hard feelings then?"

"Not now," she told him. "But the thing felt pretty hard at the time."

There was a silence and she noticed that the man was looking at her nipples. She realized that she was very flimsily dressed. The man was developing a familiar bulge in his pants.

"Well," she said, trying to be light, "what are you into tonight?"

"Just floating," he said. Regular customers were allowed to pay a floater's fee. That meant they didn't get any special woman but could partake of anything offered to them by one of the clients for that time. Or they might get off just watching the activity around the place.

"Well . . ." she said.

"Want to make some money?" he asked.

She blinked in lack of comprehension.

"I'll give you five hundred dollars if you suck my cock," he said quickly.

"What the hell would I do with money?" she asked.

He stepped in closely. "If you get enough, you can pay one of the guards to look the other way some dark night when you are ready to make a break."

Fear sent shivers down her spine. The talk was suddenly seditious and she wondered whether she might jeopardize her position just by listening to it.

"It's been done," the man urged. "If you're smart, within a year you can build quite a fortune."

Constance examined him for a long time. "Listen," she said finally. "I'll forget you said anything about escape. I work here now, so I have no reason to want to escape, you understand?" She realized that she sounded like the rankest counter-revolutionary. "But the money could be useful for other reasons."

"OK," he said, "Let's step outside."

They went out into the night air. They were in an enclosed garden surrounded by a twenty-foot wall. The man, who seemed to know the place well, took Constance by the arm and brought her behind a large shrub. When they got there, he rubbed his cock through his pants and then pulled down his zipper. There was a smutty silence in the air and she realized that she was filled with a sense of naughtiness, despite the overwhelming sexual play she had just witnessed.

"Get on your knees," the man whispered.

Constance dropped to her knees in the classic posture of submission. The man snaked his fingers into his fly and pulled his cock out. It was wrinkled and small. She took a deep breath, closed her eyes, and put the thing into her wet, hot, pretty mouth. She began sucking at once, and at once the cock began to swell. It grew proportionately larger than she had imagined and soon she was almost gagging on it. It was thick, succulent, throbbing. She forgot who it was attached to and why she was doing it, and gave herself up to the sheer sensations of the act. The earth was cool beneath her knees and the man's hands had come down to fondle her tits. She pressed in until her face was against the rough fabric of his pants. She reached behind him and cupped his buttocks, drawing him in tight. His cock slipped into her throat and abruptly, without warning, spat hot sperm down her gullet and into her belly. She found herself protesting that he had come too fast, that she was unable to savor it, and all the while swallowed as quickly as she could so she might have all the precious fluid. And then pulled back so some of it would fall on her tongue and she could enjoy the taste of it also.

He pulled back and left a trail of slimy jism on her lips. She knelt there for a few moments, rocking back and forth. The man reached into one of his pockets, pulled out five one-hundred-dollar bills, and threw them on the ground in front of her.

"Thanks, slut," he said, and sauntered off.

Constance blushed, picked up the money, put it into one of the pockets of her shorts, and left the garden. She went through the Parlor and out another door to the employees' quarters, checking past a guard who goosed her as she went by him, and then out onto the turf next to the swimming pool where she flung herself into one of the beach chairs.

Her mind was a rushing river of thoughts, for she was trying to assimilate a complete reversal of everything she had considered her standard of values for her entire life. On one level, she felt a tremendous exhilaration, probably like that of the solitary cougar padding the crags of New Mexico mountains in its hunt for the fresh kill. At that point, there is no morality, no trace of doubt, but the simple imperative of hunger and the appeasement of it in whatever way nature has provided.

But at another level, Constance felt that she had taken a step down in going from slave to employee. At least as a slave she had no boss. She could retain her inner freedom even though her body was being owned and manipulated. But when she took the step from that situation to one of staff member, she gave up some of her integrity in return for a measure of security. She opted for a longer and more comfortable life as a real slave, that is to say, a voluntary slave, instead of a brief life with extraordinary hardships but as a human being who maintained self-respect.

"Yet," she reasoned, "it's not so cut and dry. The things that were done to me in the Parlor went a long way to erode the harsh distinctions of abstract morality. And the fact that no matter how I choose I can't change the reality of the condition also helped sway me. Also, I really needed to feel a man in that way, and probably would have done anything for it."

She finally lapsed into cerebral silence and let herself enjoy the simple pleasure of lying down under the night sky. But after a few minutes, she heard a noise. She opened her eyes just in time to feel her arms being grabbed and a gag stuffed in her mouth. Four or five women swarmed over her and within seconds she was standing up, her hands tied behind her, gagged and blindfolded.

"Take her along," she heard a voice say and instantly recognized it as belonging to Madge.

She was marched for a number of minutes and finally made to sit down. Then the gag and blindfold were taken off. Madge stood in front of her and before saying a word she lifted her right hand high in the air and hit Constance a savage stinging blow across the cheek.

"Fucking traitor!" Madge hissed.

Constance's head swum. She saw nothing for half a minute but a surging sea of black dotted with white pinpricks of light. The harsh taste of blood flooded the inside of her mouth. She rocked back and forth on her seat.

"Madge," she said at last.

"Don't even dirty my name by using it, you backstabbing cunt," Madge said and raised her arm in the other direction and hit Constance again, this time backhanded.

Once again she was rocketed to the edge of unconsciousness. Everything grew black in front of her and she almost fell to the ground. Madge hit her two or three more times and Constance heard another voice say, "Take it easy."

"Take it easy, my ass," Madge exploded. "This is only warm-up, compared to what I'm going to do to her."

"But not here," the other voice said.

"It's as good a place as any," Madge said. "It's the one we agreed on. What's the matter? You getting cold feet?"

"But she's a sister." Constance now recognized the other voice as belonging to Sheila.

"Sellout sister, you mean," Madge said.

"Madge," Constance said. "Listen to me."

"Sure, I'm ready to listen," Madge said. "You got five minutes to state your case before we sentence you."

Constance tried to gather her thoughts, a difficult task under the circumstances. There was nothing she could say that would really defend her position and yet she had to try. She took an emotional tack.

"I'm as much a victim of this place as you are," she began. "And if I had a choice, I'd get out. But escape is impossible. Robert told me that they know about the gimmick of whispering to pass information during the orgies. And a lot more. Believe me, they have it all covered. They only let us think there's a way out so that we won't give in to despair and become totally useless. And then he threatened me. He told me my choice was either to become a staff member or get snuffed, that very night." This was a lie but she was in no mood to make fine distinctions. "So I told him I'd join them. But I haven't sold you out. I'm still getting information. I'm still preparing to escape. It's just that now I have better access. I can get to the guards more easily. I have money. And when I do get out, I'll come back and get you all out. You must know that."

There was a silence. Sheila finally said, "See, I told you she was still one of us. She wouldn't sell out." She turned to Constance. "Do you really have a good chance of escaping now?"

"Oh shit!" Madge said. "You don't believe her, do you? She's one of them. You can tell by the look in her eyes. And didn't she help that guy to ravish that poor girl tonight? Migene was there. She saw it."

"All I hear," said a third woman, someone Constance had never seen before and in front of whom Madge showed some deference, "is accusations and

91

denials going back and forth. As far as I'm concerned, there's no way to decide objective guilt." Constance breathed a secret sigh of relief. "But on the other hand, from a purely pragmatic viewpoint, we can't do nothing. So, on the grounds of pure expediency, I vote that we kill her."

"I second it," said Madge.

"I agree," said each of two others.

"I can't," Sheila said at last. She was trembling and close to tears. "I can't help to execute Constance. I love her."

"Then you'd better get your ass out of here," Madge said. "And let us do what is necessary."

Sheila bent down, took Constance's face between her hands, and kissed her on the mouth. "I'm sorry," she said, and then, to Constance's amazement, winked. She turned quickly and ran off.

"How shall we do it?" the first woman asked Madge.

Madge thought for a few seconds and then smiled, a frightening expression under the circumstances.

"Suffocation," she said. And then reached forward to undo the ropes. Within a few seconds, Constance was free. But then Madge twisted one arm and forced her to the ground.

"Hold her," she commanded.

Each of two women grabbed one of her wrists and held it pinned to the ground while the third woman held her ankles down. Constance was totally unable to move.

"Now," Madge said and took off her skirt and blouse. She stood there naked, her pendulous breasts swaying, her heavy haunches looking sinister as they loomed over Constance's face. She then fell to her knees, one knee at either side of Constance's head. Madge's acid-smelling bush was inches from Constance's face. Madge looked down and into Constance's eyes.

"Good-bye, sweetheart," Madge said. "I really liked you and would have loved to have you as a comrade."

Then she squatted down, bringing her buttocks over Constance's face. At first the association was with sex, her mouth being squashed by the erotic bulk. But Madge pushed down with greater weight than she would if it were truly an erotic encounter. Constance felt her nose being mashed and the heavy flesh of the buttocks totally covering her lips. She tried to take a breath and found that she couldn't! Panic seized her.

She twisted her head to one side, using all her strength, and was able to gasp in a lungful of air. But Madge pressed her thighs tight together and once again Constance's face was drowned in a sea of flesh. The texture of the pubic hair, the musty smell of Madge's asshole, the slight smear of secretions of

Madge's cunt, all became part of a surrealistic mixture as they combined to cut off life-giving air.

Constance gathered all her strength again and was able to twist her head once more, this time letting the air out of her lungs and just barely managing to take a breath. But Madge pushed down even harder, squeezed her thigh muscles even more forcefully. Constance thrashed about but couldn't get free. Her lungs started to hurt and her head began to throb. She couldn't believe that her life was actually ending in this bizarre fashion. She reached down into her most precious reserves and pulled her head away yet one more time, and was able to gulp a very tiny mouthful of air before Madge was on top of her again.

"She keeps getting free," one of the women said.

"But each time she has less energy. She's getting very tired. And soon she won't have any strength left at all. And then I'll really squeeze her head and really sit on her face and she can try all she wants she won't be able to budge at all. And then she'll be dead."

"Oh my God," Constance thought.

Then, to her blazing consternation and surprise, she felt someone playing with her nipples and cunt. It must have been Madge since she was the only woman with her hands free. Constance felt the familiar tickling going up and down her thighs and the electric coursings zinging into her breasts. Despite everything, her pussy began to lubricate and she started to have definite erotic rushes. The finger playing with her stayed at the surface and Constance pushed her hips forward, thrusting her cunt up for more penetration.

"If I'm going to die I might as well try to squeeze in one last orgasm," she thought. She realized that she was becoming delirious from lack of oxygen and, as the erotic play distracted her from the other aspects of the situation, she found that she didn't mind being murdered at all. There was something euphoric about dying in this way. It wasn't like being strangled, for there was no pain. And she got enough sporadic bites of air to keep her conscious as she slipped into the final unconsciousness. The transition was not brutally abrupt.

Now Madge pressed down with a vengeance and Constance no longer struggled. She let the thrills shoot up from her cunt into her belly. She let the ass and cunt cover her face and block out all light and air. She let herself sink, sink, sink into oblivion.

And then everything was black and she lost all awareness.

But a minute later smelling salts were being passed under her nose and someone was tapping her face lightly, exhorting her to wake up. She coughed, spluttered, and took deep, ragged breaths of air into her lungs. She burst back into life and the process was very painful. Finally, she opened her eyes and found herself looking into Robert's face.

"I think it may be more pleasant to be dead," she said.

"You almost were," he told her.

"How did you find me?"

In reply, Robert merely nodded his head. Off to one side stood Sheila looking down with fearful eyes.

"She came and got us and told us what was going on," he said.

"Sheila," Constance called out. "You saved my life."

"I couldn't let them do it," the redhead said. "I think Madge is just wicked."

Robert helped Constance to stand up. There were two attendants nearby, one of whom was Roger. He smiled and told her he was glad to see her still among them. Then Robert dismissed the two men and told Sheila that she would be contacted the next day and would probably receive placement on the staff as a reward.

Then the two of them were alone.

"It was a close call," he said.

"You actually sound concerned," she replied.

"I would have missed you very much."

"With all the women you have at your disposal?"

"You know as well as I do that special is special. You know how I feel about you."

"In normal circumstances you would probably ask me to marry you. What do you do here?"

For an answer he put his arms around her and drew her close to him. His hands slid down her back and cupped her buttocks. He pulled her tightly and she felt his cock press against her cunt. It was hot and it tingled. She tilted her face up to receive his kiss, and sighed when his tongue went into her mouth. They sank slowly to the ground together, and when they were lying side by side she unzipped his pants and took his cock in her hand. It was hot and hard and thick and she closed her eyes in pleasure at the feel of it. Luckily, she was already naked so it was easy for him to roll over onto her and slip his prick into her already sopping cunt.

"I was almost dead a few minutes ago and now I'm lying here being fucked," she thought.

She allowed herself to drift off into a revery, which detailed the strange journey she had found herself on, in the way that people often do during sex, letting the sensations of the physical serve as a kind of muted and pleasant background music to the progression of ideas. And she had quite lost herself in that process when she came to and found that she was in Robert's arms, her legs wrapped around his back, her hands in his hair, her mouth open and letting forth cries of passion. Then she was kissing him and hugging him and giving herself to him entirely, her body a rocking horse he rode, her cunt a sea he swam in, her tits a cushion for his soul.

"Oh Constance," he moaned as he fucked his rampant cock into her drooling cunt.

"Darling," she whispered to the man who had saved her life, now twice.

And they rode the wave of their excitement until it burst and he spilled his seed inside her and she sucked it into her belly and was touched by the faint biological overtone of conceiving a child in the bowels of the Slave Parlor.

They climaxed together and lay in one another's arms for a long time afterwards, even allowing themselves the luxury of slipping into sleep.

Finally, he roused himself and pulled himself from her. She smiled and stretched. She looked up at him with the delicious languor of a well-fed cat. He held down one hand and helped her to her feet. He put one arm around her and they strolled off.

"How about dinner in my room?" he asked.

"Sounds marvelous," she told him.

"And then a movie."

"Great."

"And then for a proper romp in bed. I have a cabinet full of happy pills that make what you've taken so far seem like candy bars."

"I'm due back on duty."

"No, in light of your experience, you've been given three days off."

She smiled and they walked on until, a few feet later, Constance heard the distant sound of rifles being shot off.

"What's that?" she asked.

"They've executed Madge and her cohorts," he told her.

Constance felt a sharp pain in her heart. "Madge," she said.

"Don't think about it," he counseled. "She tried to kill you. You should kill any sentimental feelings you have for her."

"I wonder if, after a while, I'll be capable of any feeling at all."

"Why should you want to be?" he asked. "Feelings only interfere with sensation."

They walked for a bit and then Constance stopped and looked around her a long time. The sky was clear. The sea was white in the moonlight. The buildings seemed to sleep. And over in the distance, she knew, the Parlor carried on its gaming, like an all-night casino.

Constance tried to remember how long she'd been there. Probably three months. It all seemed so familiar. She knew most of the faces and routines. And yet it was all so alien and distant. She still didn't know who the owners were. And it was still a situation that would have outraged her sensibilities of several months ago. Could she have changed that much?

Robert paused to stand next to her.

"What are you looking at?" he asked.

She gazed at him and then swept her glance over the entire compound.

"Home," she said, and smiled, and put her arm around his waist, and walked with him toward a night of entertainment and sensual delight.

8

"But what's wrong with having a baby?"

Constance paced up and down in front of the large bay window of the suite that she now shared with Robert. It had been six months since the fateful night on which he saved her life, and both had risen higher in the organization. Robert was now a liaison officer, which meant that he handled messages between the entire staff at the Parlor and the owners themselves. He was sworn to secrecy and could tell Constance nothing about the people he worked with, but on more than one occasion hinted that her eyes would bulge out if she had the faintest inkling who the controllers really were. He told her that he had not met with any of them personally, but through hints and deductions could guess at the identity of many of them.

"They've really covered themselves. Even if the place were busted, they would get off. The only thing I can't yet figure out is why they maintain the place to begin with. But I think it must be one of those embarrassing things, like the Vietnam War, where they just got in and don't know how to get out." That was about as much as he had been able to convey to her about the people who kept the Parlor going.

Constance had been promoted, over three stages, to the rank of activities coordinator, which meant that she took the orders, picked the girls, and made out the schedules. The two of them were given permission, as a reward, to live together. Their apartment was the envy of everyone who worked there and their occasional parties were infamous.

Now Constance turned to face Robert who was sprawled on the couch reading the copy of the *Times* that had just been flown in. He had been looking it over for half an hour, muttering that the world outside had gone mad and that he was glad to have found an asylum away from the idiocies of civilization. Constance kept trying to pull him into what had become her favorite topic.

"It's just unheard of," he finally replied. "I mean, who ever heard of having a baby in a slave colony?"

"I don't recall from any of the history I've read that people stopped having babies just because they were slaves. In fact, it seems to me that slaves reproduce more. And anyway, we're not technically slaves. We are actually employees."

"Who aren't allowed to leave."

"I imagine we could escape if we wanted to. Now."

He glanced over at her, frowning at her incursion into the forbidden topic. "I like it here," he said. "It gives me everything I want."

"All right then. If this is where we're going to settle down, then I want to have a baby."

"What about your duties?"

"I've already cleared it through channels. I can get time off during the last month of pregnancy and for the first few months after birth. And then I can set up a day-care nursery. Maybe some of the other women will want children also."

"And what happens to the child when it grows up?"

"It finds its place in the world it was born into, just like any other child."

"And do you imagine the children will have a good time playing games in the Parlor?"

"The Parlor is a fact of life," she said. "Every society has its little horror show. The only difference here is that we're more open about it, that's all."

Robert put his paper down and held out his arms. "When have I been able to deny you anything?" he said.

"Whenever you want, until I break down your resistance," she replied.

She went over and lay down next to him. She snuggled in tightly, her breasts crushing against his chest. He let his hands roam freely over her, sampling her charms for perhaps the three hundredth time, but with no loss of excitement and affection. He nibbled at her ear and licked her throat. Constance purred and pushed herself even further into him. Naked, relaxed, turned on, they gave themselves up to the leisured lovemaking that comes as a reward to those couples who have been able to get through the difficult periods of relationship to sail on a smooth sea of erotic enjoyment.

He cupped her lush buttocks and squeezed the firm flesh. She tightened her ass cheeks and pulled his fingers into her. He bent down and began to lavish the hot wet kisses of his tongue on one of her breasts, licking the nipple, which had turned purple and was already wrinkled with desire. His cock got hard and slid between her thighs, rubbing against the excitable outside lips of her hungry cunt. She straddled his cock and rubbed herself back and forth on it, humping him with growing lust.

"I didn't think we'd be doing it so soon after last night," she whispered.

The night before they had had one of their infrequent gatherings, and had two of the slave girls brought in along with three of the guards. They had decided to enact "Roman Emperor," and Robert had stretched out on their bed while the two women sucked his cock simultaneously, kissing and licking one another's mouths through the medium of his throbbing erection, their tits cradling his thighs, their asses high and hot before his eyes. And as he wallowed in the voluptuousness of surrender to their tender ministrations, he watched the show on the floor in front of him. There Constance was fucked by three men at once. They had taken her in a variety of ways. First serially, with her on her knees as one after the other of the guards mounted her from behind and fucked her dog-fashion. Then she blew each of the men, walking on her knees from man to man, wrapping her trembling and wet lips around each of their cocks. And finally, they triple-teamed her. One lay on his back and she impaled herself on his cock. The second fucked her in the ass. And the third took her mouth. And they rode her like that for an hour, stuffing her with cock, covering her with their hands and bodies. And all the while Robert watched through lidded eyes and allowed his slaves to lavish pleasure on his prick.

"Having you alone is always a treat after one of our groups," he told her.

"You know," she confessed, "whenever we start to make love I am struck by a strange thought right at the beginning. I say to myself, 'What if, suddenly, we forget how to do it? What if we lose the knack because of overdoing it so much?'"

"And then what happens?"

"And then I get a hot flash in my belly and my ass starts to move and I wonder how I got such a foolish idea in the first place."

Robert chuckled and gathered her in more tightly to himself. He pulled her under him and hoisted himself on top so that he was lying with his full weight on her. She parted her legs and he tilted his pelvis and his cock head came directly into contact with the opening of her cunt. She bit her lip as he entered her, his cock sliding slow and full into the hot, wet recesses of her pussy.

"A rare treat, my dear," he said. "A good, old-fashioned fuck in the classic missionary position."

Her legs rose in the air and spread apart. He aimed his cock like a spear and sunk himself into her very core. Her cunt went soft and squishy and she pushed it against him, rippling the inner muscles. It almost felt as though it would turn inside out in its engulfing need to spread apart and swallow him. The odor of her secretions was already filling the room like the smell of orchids in a hothouse.

"Ohhhh," she moaned. "Ohhhh, drive it deep. Fill me up. Shove your cock all the way up into my belly."

She grabbed the backs of her knees and pulled her legs even more widely apart. She was split apart like a log that had just been cleft by an axe. Her whole body was trembling, her tits jiggling, her mouth open and wet. She clenched her thighs and pumped her ass and tried to pull him entirely inside her. He rode her with wild dispassion, totally involved and yet at a distance, enjoying not only his own sensations but vicariously grooving on the effect he was having on her.

"Fuck me like a sow in heat," she grunted. "Fuck me hard."

He began to buck into her, pile-driving his stiff rod into her tender and spongy cunt. She let out a series of high-pitched moans, going wild with the rough handling her pussy was receiving. She had her fingers dug into his back, the nails breaking the skin, causing little rivulets of blood to run down between his shoulder blades. As he fucked her, she sailed off into a spectacular reverie, seeing all at once the universal and varied fucking that was taking place all over the world. She pictured the rooms of the buildings in the compound, the attendants popping happy pills, the slave women in their lesbian orgies, the bizarre carryings-on in the Parlor. She saw fists going into cunts, into assholes. She saw women drinking piss. Everywhere there was a rain of cock and pussy, tits and ass, gulping mouths and lapping tongues.

"Oh fuck, fuck, fuck," she cried out. And at precisely that instant, Robert climaxed, shudders running up and down his spine, his buttocks quivering, the sperm splashing from his cock into the waiting walls of Constance's cunt.

"Oh yes, yes!" she cried. "Give it to me. Give me your cum. Give me your baby."

And she glued her body to his, sucking the last drops of sperm from his cock with her cunt, grasping him, pulling at him, milking him dry, until he lay on her spent and exhausted, an emptied vessel, a tool that had served its purpose.

"I think we did it," she said after a long while. "I really felt it. I felt you shoot it up into my womb."

"It will be interesting," was all he could get it together to say.

He began to rouse himself to reach for a cigarette when all of a sudden all of the alarm bells in the compound went off at once. It was as though an airplane had suddenly come crashing out of the sky and exploded right in their middle. Constance felt her heart stop with fear. The very floor seemed to shake with the vibration.

"What is it?" she gasped.

"A raid," he said. "We're being raided."

"But I thought this place was invulnerable."

"Politics keep shifting," he said. "Maybe it's suddenly become in the interest of the owners to have the scene busted up."

"What can we do?" she asked.

"There's a secret passageway," he told her. "We have to get dressed very quickly, get our money stash, and try to get out before we're caught."

Even in the midst of the emergency, Constance had a moment for a fleeting smile. "That's what I like about you, Robert," she said. "You never get lost in subtleties."

He was already putting his pants and shirt on and urging her to do the same when they heard the sound of gunfire. The guards were fighting off whichever force it was that was invading. Constance pulled on a pair of slacks and a shirt. They put on shoes, dug out a small leather pouch that held money and traveling essentials, and went out a back door behind the false wall at the back of the clothes closet.

They fled down a long hallway and came at last to a small door. They yanked it open and stepped out into the middle of the jungle, which started right outside the compound. Robert had a map and a compass in the pouch, and they planned to wend their way to a village and move out from there. But the minute they straightened up and stepped into the sunlight, they realized that the game was up. Four men in grey business suits holding automatic pistols were standing there waiting for them.

"FBI," one of the men said. "Don't move."

They swooped down and frisked the two of them, relieving them of their pouch. Robert and Constance were told to put their hands on their heads and to march back through the tunnel. They moved slowly and finally got back into their room where several other agents had already arrived from the other direction. Constance glanced out the window and saw that the compound was swarming with men in grey business suits. They were surrounded by hordes of slave girls who were jumping up and down in glee, ready to give their all to their rescuers. But most of them were either naked or dressed in the scantiest of clothing, and the fact that they were ready to drop to their knees and suck the cocks of the agents seemed the most normal thing in the world to them; they had lost touch with the reality of the outside world in which such things weren't thought, much less done.

"They are going to have a harder time adjusting back to their old lives than they can begin to imagine," Constance thought. "And what about me? I ought to be with them, one of the women freed from the tyranny of her captors. And yet, here I am, being treated as a prisoner. Will I be put on trial? Will I be arrested? Will I go to prison?" As the questions bounced back and forth across her mind, she was already beginning to write the story, figuring out how she might escape the censure of the law.

It would be difficult for her to plead innocence. Too many of the other women knew of her status, had seen her in the Parlor, had joined her in her quarters for wild parties. Constance also had the files of all the slaves and customers in her office, and it would be easy for any prosecutor to prove that she was a kind of Eichmann of the Slave Parlor.

"Take him out," one of the agents said. Robert had a gun poked in his back and was led from the room. As he reached the door, he turned to Constance, smiled, and winked. She doubted she would ever see him again. She was convinced he would find some way to kill himself before he allowed himself the ignominy of a public trial. Her eyes misted over as she watched what could easily be the father of the child she was certain she had just conceived walk out of her life forever.

When he was gone, there were five agents left in the room. The one in charge sent two others out on an errand, and when the door had closed she was left with the three remaining men. It didn't take but a split second for her to realize just what they had in mind.

"We have about twenty minutes," the one in charge said.

"Will we be disturbed?" the second one asked.

"No, this sector is secure and no one will enter without contacting me first." He flourished his walkie-talkie.

"So the cunt is all ours for twenty minutes," the second one went on.

"Take your clothes off, bitch," the man in charge told Constance.

She balked for an instant and the third man came up behind her and cuffed her ears. Her head rang with the blow and she staggered forward.

"Off with 'em, cunt," the first man repeated.

Constance trembled. Never had she been so repulsed and frightened. Even when tied to a table, blindfolded and gagged, with a strange man fist-fucking her, she had never felt the level of repulsion she now experienced. There was something brutal about these men that surpassed anything she had ever encountered. She tried to figure out what it was as she slipped out of her pants, exposing her pretty and delicate ass to their hot eyes, letting them have access to her cunt; she speculated on what the insight might mean as she shrugged out of her blouse, letting her tits fall free. In a few seconds she was standing stark naked in the middle of the triangle formed by the three agents.

Then she saw what it was. All the other men, no matter how brutal, had been straightforward. But these men were wallowing in hypocrisy. Supposedly dedicated to eradicating crime, they never took an issue to its root. They wouldn't dream of going after the real owners. Constance was sure that the young psychopath who had hung her over a cliff would not be bothered by the agents. They would only go after small fry and medium fry, and in the process take whatever advantage they could.

"Nice piece of ass," one of the men commented. "Ain't she the one that got kidnapped after writing the story?"

"Yeah," the second man replied. "And then she sold out."

"Oooh, let me at her," the third man said.

And for the next fifteen minutes she became a pin cushion for their cocks. They bent her over and fucked her from behind, and forced her mouth, and took her two at a time. She took the indignities in stride, having reached the point where hardly anything men did to her could upset her in any meaningful fashion. But just as she was beginning to pull her awareness back from the activity in and around her, she felt something hard and cold at her temple. One of the agents was holding a gun to her head.

"Now we'll see how much cool this cunt has," the agent said. And then to Constance. "I want to see you give the best blow job that anybody has ever given," he told her. "And if you miss one stroke, I'm going to put a bullet through your head and you'll be listed as having tried to escape."

Having her brains blown out by an FBI agent was definitely not the way Constance wanted to die, so she put all her effort into the task. On her knees in traditional cocksucking style, her hands wrapped around the man's cock, she stuffed the rod of meat into her mouth and started sucking. She licked and pulled, slobbered and moaned. She worked until she was drooling and her hair was flying like mad around her eyes. The three men glared down at her, their mouths split into smiles.

When they had received the assignment, the director had told them that they were going into one of the most vile rackets that had ever existed on earth, and that they were not to spare anyone connected with the slave ring. They couldn't kill indiscriminately, but on the other hand, they didn't need to be too nice about how they handled those they captured. Their major concerns were two: to secure the release of the innocent victims and to keep their hands off all the owners, if such were even to be found on the grounds. Thus, they knew they had carte blanche with Constance and immensely enjoyed the spectacle of her sucking cock to save her life.

"Oooh, I'm coming," the man groaned. "Swallow it, swallow it!" He put his hands on Constance's head and forced her face to burrow deeply into his crotch until her mouth was buried in his pubic hair. And when he came, his sperm spurted onto the back of her tongue and splashed down her throat. She swallowed it with huge gulps, indicating how much she relished the load being pumped into her face.

"Time's up," the man in charge said. "Maybe we can take another crack at her later."

Off in the distance there were the sounds of helicopters, seaplanes, tanks. The army of the local dictator, having been alerted, was now roaring in. Although the dictator knew of and got revenue from the Parlor, he now had to pretend that the existence of such a place was a total scandal and shock. The attack on the Parlor, spearheaded by the FBI, was now to include police and military. Soon after, reporters would arrive, and a whole slew of lawyers, muckrakers, writers, television, radio, film, and the whole scavenging crew of media coverage.

Constance was yanked to her feet. She wiped her mouth with the back of her hand and tried to put her hair back in place. They allowed her to get dressed, although their hands were all over her as she pulled her clothes back on, and they stroked and pinched and prodded her tits and ass and cunt continually. Finally, she was ready, and they pushed her out into the front hallway, and took her down to the courtyard, which was being set up as a detention center.

There she saw all her collaborators, the attendants, the guards who hadn't been killed, the maids, the upper-echelon executives. They all looked dejected and crestfallen. They could all look forward to very long prison sentences, probably life. She was pushed into the crowd and she milled around a bit, exchanging words of encouragement with the others.

"Oh, if I hadn't gone over to the other side," she said to herself. "This would be a day of liberation for me."

And then the idea hit her. She hadn't gone over to the other side, she had been forced. They had used drugs, and threats, and hypnosis, and extreme erotic experiences to break her will, and after a while she didn't know what she was doing. In fact, she had had amnesia for much of the time. And wasn't aware of her behavior.

"I wonder if I can get away with that story," she thought.

She reasoned that she could. If Robert did commit suicide, there would be no immediate voice to be raised against her, although she was certain he would back her up if she tried to cop a plea. The records in her office were

104

impersonal enough. And the testimony of the slave girls could be nullified if she could convince a jury that she was indeed out of her mind when she joined the staff.

What astonished her was the realization that she was going into much more of a state of shock in reentering the world at large than she had when she was first taken into the Parlor. She marveled at how much she had changed. She had killed a man, had seen a good friend shot because of an attempt on her own life, had fallen in love with a brutal killer, had indulged in dozens of lesbian orgies, had been fist-fucked, pissed on, whipped, and sold herself for money scores of times. And now she was a hardened bureaucrat in a slave empire, hoping that she was pregnant. And with all this she was expected to go back into the world of civil appearances. It was ludicrous.

"Well, one thing's for sure. I'm not going to go to prison if I can help it. I'll lie and cheat and do what I have to, to keep out of jail."

It was just as she was lost in the middle of these ramblings that she heard her name called out. "Constance, Constance," a male voice repeated several times. For a few seconds she thought it was Robert. But when she turned in the direction of the sound, she saw a stranger coming toward her. It was a man she didn't recognize, although he seemed to know her for he called her name and waved and smiled and seemed exceedingly glad to see her.

He was within five feet of her before she knew who it was.

"Chet!" she exclaimed.

"Darling," he said and threw his arms around her.

But at just that instant one of the agents stepped forward and brusquely pulled them apart.

"What the fuck . . . ?" Chet exclaimed.

"Sorry, no contact is allowed with the prisoners," the agent said.

"Prisoners?" Chet yelled. "What the hell are you talking about? This is the woman who led to the breakup of the ring. She was the one who discovered the kidnappings and helped me break the code of their pattern."

"I don't know anything about that," the agent said. "She was found in the employees' section, living with one of the bigwigs. And I understand she had a pretty important job here herself."

Chet stared at her. He was taller than she remembered, and there was a look of vulnerability in his eyes that she had forgotten could exist in a man. He looked like a puppy dog that had just been capriciously whipped by its master.

"Is that true?" he whispered.

"Chet, it's not what he's making it out to be. They were going to kill me. I had to find some way to stay alive. You have no idea. They kept us drugged and whipped and continually toyed with our lives. I pretended

105

to go over just to save my skin. And I was able to help a lot of the girls that way. Ask them."

Chet took one long hard look at her and knew that she was lying. She knew that he knew. She had forgotten just how well he knew her. There was no way that she could fool him. The entire story of her betrayal was written in her eyes, and he could read her eyes the way one could read a book. Then the awareness of what had happened struck her.

"Chet, you led them here," she said.

He nodded. "I went to the FBI. And showed them my tapes. It wasn't too hard to piece together the next location and time of a kidnapping. Then they put a woman agent in the way of the slavers, and by the fifth town they were able to have her kidnapped. She was brought here and sent out a message by means of a special transmitting device. Then the bureau had to plan its attack, coordinate with the local government. And from what I understand, some pretty big people are mixed up in this thing, so they had to find out which toes not to step on. And . . . well, here we are."

The two of them were silent for a long time. All around them the hubbub continued. The inpouring of the soldiers who were just learning what kind of a place it was and who looked at the slave women with lust and envy, wishing they could drop their guise of good guys and just indulge in some good old-fashioned raping and pillaging. The FBI men scurried about like ants.

"And you," he asked. "What happened to you?" And his tone of voice demanded the truth.

"I don't want to go to prison," she said.

"You know I'll help you all I can," he told her. "But I have to have the truth from your own mouth."

"All right," she told him, and the two of them stepped aside, out of hearing of the agent.

"It was a shock," she said. "To wake up captured, bound, and gagged, with some strange man fucking me. And on top of that, to be enjoying it. Then the slow realization that I would never escape. I had to come to terms with the possibility that I would die here. And it could come any time. From time to time the girls were called for a Snuff, and sooner or later it would have been my turn. Then I met Robert, and he made me fall in love with him. He used every trick in the book, threatening my life one moment and making delicious sex the next. And so I succumbed, I gave myself to him. Then he offered to put me on staff, and I had no real alternative. I couldn't escape, and all that was left was to spend three or four sessions in the Parlor every week until I was too scarred and used for anything but to be killed by a strange man. I couldn't face that. So I went over to the other side."

106

Chet didn't say anything for a long time. A universe of feeling went through him, and when he finally did speak it was with great suppressed emotion.

"You know that I love you. And my stomach churns when I think of the things that were done to you, and when I think of you loving another man in the same way you loved me. But I'll stand by you and maybe I can help to get you free."

They stared at one another over the distance between them, the gap that they couldn't cross. The guard would not let them embrace, and even had they been able to physically hold one another, they would have found high walls inside themselves, holding them back from a total and complete giving to one another.

Constance gazed on the second man in her life and pondered at the mysteries of love. Chet was good and kind and gentle and patient. He wanted marriage and children and continuity. While Robert was cruel and capricious and sharp. He wanted nothing but ever more exquisite sensations, even when they were purchased at the cost of causing another person to suffer. And yet she loved each of them, each in a different way, each with a different aspect of totality.

She put her hands on her belly and tried to feel the miracle that had just taken place there. She was convinced that Robert's seed was at this very instant burying itself in the egg that clung to the walls of her womb. And in the face of that, she was going to go out into the world, to face possible imprisonment.

Just then she heard a loud uproar and hubbub coming from behind the swimming pool. Voices shouting, people running. There was no way to tell what was going on for a while, and she and Chet remained in silence, looking at one another, trying to salvage the reality of their former lives from the wreckage of the present.

Their concentration was interrupted by an agent who came up to her and said, "Excuse me, is your name Constance?"

"Yes," she told him.

"There's a man named Robert who broke away from his guards and is standing at the edge of the cliff," the Agent went on. "We're trying to talk him down but he insists on seeing you."

"Robert!" she thought and a thrill ran through her. She looked up at Chet, but he had already seen the effect the news had had on her.

"I'm sorry," he said. "I will help you all I can, but I guess I have to accept the fact that this man is very, very important to you."

"Oh thank you, darling," she said. "I so need your understanding now." And then, turning to the agent, "Please, take me to him."

The place was already beginning to be flooded with waves of normality. The FBI agents had reached a point where they were beginning to be concerned about someone's life. They were coming down off the terrific high they received when first stumbling into the Parlor. The soldiers were starting to act in an orderly fashion. Soon, the buildings would be emptied, and the machinery of civilization installed, and the Parlor would have become a memory and a scandal, and within a year leave no trace.

The agent took Constance to where Robert was. He was perched at the very edge of the cliff, standing with complete insouciance, looking down. He held his life in his hands and so was utterly invulnerable to anything anyone else might try to do to him. It was only when he saw Constance that his spine stiffened and he seemed to take some interest in his surroundings.

"See if you can talk to him," the agent said, betraying that fear and loathing of suicide, which daunts even the most calloused of men.

He let go of her arm for an instant, thinking that she would take one or two steps forward to talk to Robert, but at precisely that moment she broke loose and ran as fast as she could to Robert, to fly in his arms and stand with him at the very brink of the precipice.

"Darling," he said.

"They wanted me to talk you out of jumping," she said.

"And you? What do you want?"

"I want you to take me with you," she said.

He smiled. "Good girl," he told her. "I knew you wouldn't take the easy way out."

"They have nothing to offer me now," she said. "Trial, degradation, newspapers, prison. And even if I beat the rap, to spend the rest of my life in that tawdry, mediocre world. I couldn't. I've flown too high and sunk too low to ever be satisfied with plodding along on the ground again."

"Come back," they heard a voice say. It was the agent. He seemed absurd, with his tight suit and his worried expression, waving at them. They both laughed.

Then, at the edge of the crowd, Constance saw Chet, and she stiffened momentarily. Robert, to whom she had told the story of her former lover, saw him also.

"Is that Chet?" he asked.

"Yes," she whispered.

"He's the one who led them to us?"

"Yes. He meant well. He still does. But Chet will never stop plodding. I love him dearly, but he doesn't make my soul sing."

Robert put his arm around her shoulders and the two of them turned their backs to the crowd and looked out toward the sea. The sun was setting. It was a calm, warm afternoon. The water was orange and red and yellow with the dying light. From far below they could hear the surf pounding. They looked down. Jagged rocks gleamed amidst the spumes of swirling foam.

"I wonder what it will feel like," she said.

"That's what everybody wants to know. And we don't find out until it's too late to tell anyone else. The secret is very well kept."

He slid his arm down and ran his hand over her ass. She twitched her buttocks. "Please, Robert," she said. "Not here. Everyone's looking."

"Come back. We want to talk to you!" the voice of the agent rang out again. Robert and Constance pretended they didn't hear.

"Would you care to go for a swim, my dear?" he asked.

She looked over at him, her expression a perfect mixture of fear and joy.

"I'd go anywhere with you, and do anything," she said.

He began to unbutton his shirt and she joined him in taking her own clothes off. Within half a minute, they were both naked. Then he took her in his arms and held her tightly. She raised her face up and their mouths met. Their kiss was long and deep and passionate.

"Good-bye, Constance," a voice rang out. It was Chet. Without looking up she waved one hand at him.

She could feel Robert's cock, now hard, pressing between her thighs. She raised her right leg and brought it around his waist, opening her cunt up for him to enter. He bent his knees a fraction and brought his cock up from underneath, sliding it into the split cunt. She gasped. Then she brought her other leg up and wrapped that around him so that she was totally off the ground, her legs around his waist, her cunt gulping his cock.

Behind them they could hear whistles and applause from the gathered crowd. They had become such a spectacle that all discipline had broken down, and FBI agents and soldiers and ex-slave girls and employees of the Parlor all mingled together.

Constance felt a great surge of warmth in her chest, an explosion of searing radiance in her head, and a deep pulsing in her cunt. She opened her eyes and found herself looking into Robert's soul. He had the same look of easy insouciance he always carried.

Then they were off the edge. They clung to one another tightly. The wind rushed past. The sea loomed larger and larger. Constance was laughing, she was having an orgasm. Robert smiled.

And when they smashed into the rocks, they did not lose their embrace but were totally and permanently mashed into one another, their bodies becoming indistinguishable from each other.

Then they fell into the sea. The waters covered over them. And they entered a realm of eternal and infinite peace.

109

About the Author

Marco Vassi was, without a doubt, the foremost erotic writer of our generation. Praised by Norman Malier, Kate Millett, Saul Bellow, and Gore Vidal, he was not only the ultimate sexual explorer, but a literary craftsman whose own life experiences became the stuff of his fiction—expanded, of course, by a grand imagination and a full sense of the absurd.

Tragically, Vassi died from pneumonia after he had contracted AIDS.

OPEN ROAD

INTEGRATED MEDIA

Open Road Integrated Media is a digital publisher and multimedia content company. Open Road creates connections between authors and their audiences by marketing its ebooks through a new proprietary online platform, which uses premium video content and social media.